FIGHTING TENDERFOOT

After six months in the Triangle B saddle it appeared to Webb Bannister that he was getting nowhere with his outfit, especially with Pete Hogan, the foreman. His father, the Old Man, had thrown a mighty big shadow and no one expected Webb to measure up to his standards. The day came when Webb was forced to take a stand against the rustlers who were making inroads on his cattle. Eventually, with a six-gun in his fist, Webb proved that he was capable of standing on his own feet when it seemed that everyone had turned against him.

Dún Laoghaire-Rathdown
County Council Comhairle Contae
Dhún Laoghaire-Ráth an Dúin

www.dlrcoco.ie/library

Public Library Service
Seirbhís Leabharlainne Poiblí

FIGHTING TENDERFOOT

by

Ross Harlan

Dales Large Print Books
Long Preston, North Yorkshire,
BD23 4ND, England.

British Library Cataloguing in Publication Data.

Harlan, Ross
    Fighting Tenderfoot.

    A catalogue record of this book is
    available from the British Library

    ISBN   978-1-84262-540-8 pbk

First published in Great Britain in 1992 by Robert Hale Limited

Copyright © Ross Harlan 1992

Cover illustration © Gordon Crabb by arrangement with
Alison Eldred

The right of Ross Harlan to be identified as the author of this
work has been asserted by him in accordance with the
Copyright, Designs and Patents Act, 1988

Published in Large Print 2007 by arrangement with
Robert Hale Ltd.

Dales Large Print is an imprint of Library Magna Books Ltd.

Printed and bound in Great Britain by
T.J. (International) Ltd., Cornwall, PL28 8RW

ONE

A quarter-mile from the old Silver Creek site Webb Bannister slowed his big sorrel to a walk. At a point where the trail left the edge of the woods to drop to the grass flats where the ramshackle buildings stood, he turned aside, skirting the trees and reaching the creek a hundred yards upstream.

Here he could see the homestead clearly in the afternoon sunlight. He noted a couple of ground-hitched horses, six or seven head of scrawny cattle. There was even a wired run where the hens he had heard did their clucking and squawking. But they simply flew over the wire when something caught their fancy in the open. Next, he spotted an old ranch wagon with the empty shafts tilted upwards.

Pete had been right after all, and there really was a family squatting on the old place. Well, there was only one thing he could do about it – go and tell them who owned this pocket of grass and the sprawl of buildings that had lain empty for years.

Webb put the sorrel along the creek, selecting a path around the cottonwoods and willows. He reached a bend where the water ran shallow and clean, and came up short with a low whistle leaving his lips.

The girl was wearing Levi Strauss pants and a red hickory shirt, open at the neck the way a man would wear it, and from the height of his saddle he could see the roundness of her throat dipping on to a golden swell. Her hair was gold as well, the long tresses gathered and held at the nape of her neck by a length of blue ribbon. She had been kneeling by the water, soaping a dress from a can, her smooth, tanned arms bare to the elbows.

She soon realized that she was being observed and suspended her scrubbing to regard him from level, blue eyes in which lurked suspicion and annoyance.

'Why are you gaping at me?' she demanded.

Webb swallowed and touched the brim of his hat. 'You must forgive me, miss, if you thought I was gaping.'

'But of course you were! You still are. Don't tell me you've never seen a girl before in your life?'

A faint grin relieved the sternness at

Webb's mouth. He inclined his head, hoping to take a little of the stiffness out of the situation. 'Plenty of girls.' And added, boldly: 'Not many as pretty as you, though.'

'Save your compliments for whoever will be flattered by them,' she retorted. 'And needs them.'

With this rebuff she went on washing the dress, for some minutes completely absorbed in the task. Presently she looked sideways at him. A strand of hair had escaped from the coil and fallen on to her forehead. She blew it off.

'Are you still there?'

'That's hardly a friendly welcome,' Webb chuckled. His grin widened. The girl had spirit all right, plenty of it. And she appeared to be carrying a tree-sized chip on her shoulder over something or other.

'It's not meant to be friendly,' she flashed back. 'So don't strain yourself. Pass on, cowboy.'

'Hardly the sort of talk a lonesome rider would expect,' Webb lamented. He raised his shoulders in a shrug. 'But then, some folks are just naturally friendly, and some just naturally ain't.'

'You're learning pretty fast, mister.'

The dress was thoroughly soaped and

scrubbed. She dipped it into the creek, but in so doing she overbalanced slightly and let go of the garment. The current caught it and whipped it away towards the middle of the stream.

'Oh, my dress!'

Webb came out of his saddle quickly and waded into the water. It rose to his knees. He retrieved the dress and brought it to the bank, handing it to the girl.

'Thanks, mister.'

'Don't mention it.'

He sat down and pulled his boots off to drain them. He grimaced as he tugged them back on.

'Now you've got your feet wet...'

'Wouldn't be the first time. Ain't nearly as bad as drowning.'

'I bet you were just hoping for a chance like that to make me feel obliged to you,' she accused.

Webb glared at her and a retort rose to his lips. But what was the use? He released a tight breath.

'Just forget it.'

At that moment a voice hailed from the ramshackle house. 'Reen!'

'Coming, Dad.'

She wrung her dress out and started away

through the grass towards the clutter of buildings. She didn't bother to look at Webb again. He spoke after her.

'As a matter of fact, Miss, I want to speak to you about–'

'Oh, come and eat supper with us if you're feeling cut up and hungry,' she shouted over her shoulder, adding with a laugh that was tinged with scorn: 'If you're willing to run the risk of Dad shooting you on sight.'

Webb watched her gain the rickety veranda and go on into the house. He grabbed the sorrel's bridle and led it across the front yard, draping the reins over its face.

The three steps creaked in different keys as he climbed them. He was met in the doorway by a frosty-eyed man of about sixty who had long, grizzled locks and a narrow, bony jawline. He held a Colt Peacemaker in his right hand with the muzzle levelled on the newcomer's midriff.

'What do you want?' he growled irascibly.

Webb stifled an impulse to bat the gun from him and bawl out both father and daughter. Instead, he said in a measured tone: 'Your daughter invited me to eat. But if you've got objections...'

'Ahuh! Another smart-aleck leather-slap-per? Can't say but you ain't a mite cleaner looking than most, though. But don't take that for a guarantee one way or the other. Any rattlesnake's got a nice looking skin. Come in.'

Wonderingly, and with a tingle of anxiety running along his spine, Webb allowed himself to be led through the small kitchen into the living-room. It was three months since he had been this far south: not since they had gone after the last bunch of rustlers, but the change that had been wrought made him emit that low whistle again.

Gone was the dust and the dirt and the empty cans, and the various other items of rubbish left by nomadic riders who had found the derelict homestead a convenient place to spend a day or to. The whole house had been transformed, cleaned and washed and sweetened somehow, until it was scarcely recognizable. The one window that boasted glass was now hung with chintz curtains. The others, that had been open eyes on the day and night, were neatly boarded. The make-shift furniture had been repaired, renewed, and scrubbed.

They were regarding him closely at this juncture and noticed the surprise in his eyes. They misinterpreted his expression.

'Looks better on the inside than it does on

the outside, don't it?' the girl's father commented.

'You bet.' Webb took a chair and the girl gave him a long, cool look before going into the kitchen.

'The name's Josh Parker,' the old-timer introduced himself. 'That's my daughter, Maureen.'

'Folks call me Webb.'

'Whatever you say, boy.'

Parker had tucked the Colt away under his belt. He called through to the girl: 'Vittles soon be fixed, Reen?'

'Won't take long, Dad.'

When the food was ready, Parker invited him to sit down with them. The girl laid out a large bowl of beef, potatoes and vegetables. The father dug in first. The girl helped herself next, not looking at the visitor. Webb forked a lump of beef and several potatoes on to his plate. There was certainly an appetizing odour in the air.

'Prime vegetables,' he remarked presently to the girl. 'Good cooking.' He smiled tentatively.

She gave him stony regard, saying nothing. He noted that she had fastened the neck button of the shirt and smoothed the collar down. The fugitive tendril of hair was back

13

across her forehead.

'Last season's harvesting,' Parker explained with pride in his voice. 'Toted 'em all the way from–'

'Dad!'

'Shucks, honey, let me talk if I want. But once I get that patch at the back turned over and some chicken stuff dug in... Chicken manure makes life for vegetables, mister. Did you know that?'

'New one on me, Mr Parker. But then I never had much use for digging and such.'

He caught the girl's bleak look and knew he had committed an error in making clear the difference between them. He was plainly and simply a cowman, a herder – disparagingly referred to as a cowboy. These people were hoemen, or dirt farmers, a race that the cattlemen held in contempt and treated for the most part with disdain. They weren't the only family squatting on cow graze either. Which wouldn't be so bad if they didn't have this notion that a Triangle B steer was theirs for the taking when they ran short of meat.

From that point on, the girl's attitude grew more hostile. This was conveyed in the way she rebuffed all Webb's attempts at friendly conversation.

Parker appeared to remain untouched by

the strain, or if he was aware of the tension he placidly ignored it. Parker was the sort who could turn a blind eye to lots of things. He talked about the effects of different climates on different crops and then went on blithely about rearing chickens and hogs.

Webb pretended to listen, but he was really trying to assess the two, decide who they really were and where they had hailed from; if they lived here on their own. Something persuaded him to doubt this. There was altogether too much evidence of a man's work about the place; certainly not Parker's. Josh wouldn't have the skill and the sheer vigour to bring about the changes that had been accomplished. Or would he, he asked himself, attempting to see behind the screen of verbiage the nester was throwing up.

Webb began to dread the moment when he would have to declare his identity and reveal the real nature of his visit.

When the meal was over the girl said bluntly:

'Well, I suppose Mr Webb is anxious to be on his way, Dad...'

'Not overly,' Webb cut in quickly. 'You see, I – uh...' He floundered and the girl's eye fastened on him with the intensity of a hawk on its chosen prey.

15

Parker had tamped tobacco into the bowl of a corncob pipe, he made a careless gesture that was designed to put his visitor at ease.

'Not every day I get the chance to talk to a young fella about the right way to grow things. Now, coming back to the hogs I intend to run here, mister...'

'Just a moment, Dad,' Maureen said in a peremptory manner. 'You've been running on so well that you've overlooked the fact that Mr Webb wants to get a word in. And when I come to think of it, Mr Webb, what were you doing riding along by the creek?'

Webb became aware of a wave of heat rising through his cheeks. How could he state his mission now without causing offence to the old-timer and his daughter? He had sat at their table, eaten their food. Now he must tell them to get off the Silver Creek site and find somewhere else to live.

He could see how they were waiting patiently for his answer.

'I – ah – that is, I was just drifting this way for a look at the country when I–'

'You 'pear to behaving some trouble with your tongue, Mr Webb,' Parker observed casually through a cloud of grey smoke. 'Happen you maybe got a piece of beef caught in your teeth?'

16

'Could happen, he's too scared to speak his mind honestly,' Maureen amended tartly. 'He's a cowman, isn't he? He might work for one of the outfits about here that are chasing nesters off with their tails between their legs. Don't you see, Dad, you're treating him like a friend while he might really be our enemy.'

'Hard words, honey,' Parker chided. 'If a man intended sticking a knife in your back he'd hardly sit to table and share your vittles friendly like and gabbing some.'

'You were doing the gabbing, Dad. Mr Webb here was listening.' Maureen's eyes glinted angrily. 'See how he's beginning to get red behind the ears.'

'If you'll give me a chance to explain...' Webb began. He stopped speaking as the sound of hoof-beats coming along the creek trail reached their ears.

Parker drew the Colt from his belt and rose from his chair. He placed his pipe on a plate and turned to the doorway. But the girl had reached it first, Webb close on her heels. This would be Pete, likely, Webb thought. Pete and some of the boys. Still, he had told Pete to stay away from the creek until he had visited the family.

'It's Jim,' the girl called from the veranda.

'And he has two men with him.'

Webb moved until he stood at the girl's side. He watched the horsemen angle out from the creek and come on to the front of the house at a trot. The slim, fair-haired one in the lead called to the girl.

'Howdy, Reen. I'm back, and I've brought—' He saw Webb and bit the rest off. Then, gruffly, while his blue eyes smouldered. 'Who's this?'

'Don't ask me,' Maureen replied coolly. 'He happened along and got himself invited to supper.'

'A stranger? You're crazy, Reen. Why, he might be one of that—'

Jim stopped speaking once more. He was lean and well-muscled, with the girl's flashing eyes and clean-cut features. He would be as tall as Webb on the ground, and was dressed in rough, knee-patched levis and faded grey cotton shirt. A battered sombrero that had once been a cream shade, but which had been stained and weathered to a nondescript colour, was perched on the back of his head. Hair like the girl's stuck out in unruly fashion at his neck and ears.

His companions were typical cow-country wolves, lean, ragged, wiry, dark of face, cold-eyed. They studied Webb with sullen suspicion and not a little consternation. All three were mounted on shaggy ponies, bony and fleet-looking.

Jim came out of leather in a lithe motion and strode forward until he could look directly into Webb's face. 'Who are you?' he demanded with deceptive softness while his eyes glittered like sunlight falling on coloured glass.

'Hold on, boy,' his father interposed. 'His name is Webb, and he dropped past for a bite and a chat.'

'Shut up, Dad.'

'Hey, watch who you're talking to Jim,' his father admonished. 'And mind your manners in front of all these folks.'

Jim uttered a mild oath. His gaze clung to Webb Bannister, ran over him, took in every detail of his dress, his good boots, the six-shooter lying snugly at his right hip. The flat lips curled.

'Cowman all right,' he observed in the way he might have uttered another oath. He made a jerking motion with his thumb. 'Time to get moving on, mister.'

Webb turned slowly to the girl Maureen. There was a look of devilish expectancy on her face, of gloating almost. It said that Webb had run into someone as big as himself and with as much nerve, and she was curious to see how he would react. Anger caused his throat to constrict for a moment and he swallowed hard.

'Don't worry,' he said to Jim. 'I was just leaving anyway.'

He descended the three steps, Jim stalking him like a cougar, saying with thinly-veiled scorn: 'And don't come back again too soon. We don't hanker after your sort here.'

Webb halted at that, studied the toe of his left boot for an instant, then swung about. His features were expressionless as he looked from the man to his sister; he allowed a thin smile to pucker his mouth.

'So long anyhow, Miss. Watch your dress don't fall into the water again.'

He moved away, but Jim's blunt fingers fastened on his shoulder, dug in, and drew him around on his heels.

'What in hell do you mean by that, mister?'

'Nothing at all,' Webb responded coolly. 'Your sister knows what I'm talking about.'

'I see! Then it's time I knew as well. Cough up, Mr Webb, or you'll find yourself in bother right *pronto*.'

Webb braced himself, measured the man. The other two, who had remained mounted, were grinning widely now, savouring the situation, eager to see the cowman brought to heel. The girl came down the steps into the yard. She looked suddenly worried. 'Never mind him, Jim. Just let him be.'

'Shut up, Reen. Let me handle what I start.'

He touched Webb's chest with the tips of his fingers in a light, pushing motion. Webb refused to budge under the pressure.

'Get going, mister.'

'In a minute, mister.'

Webb hit him, his right fist swinging up with all his strength and concentrated fury behind it. It connected with the tip of Jim's chin and sent him reeling off balance. He teetered wildly, lost his footing, and fell heavily to the hard earth.

He was up in a moment, crouching, shoulders hunched, arms in front of him, fists balled. The girl shouted: 'Jim, stop it!'

Jim growled wrathfully and rushed Webb. Webb swerved aside, then slammed a full-blooded straight left into his ribs as he rushed past. Jim went to his knees, hunched there while he dragged air to his lungs. When he charged Webb again he was met with a rain of blows delivered mercilessly. Twice only did Jim succeed in breaking through Webb's guard and catching him on the left cheek and mouth.

Webb felt blood trickle over his chin, but he didn't mind; he was scarcely aware of the blows having landed. A final looping left deposited the breathless Jim on his back in the yard. This time he was in no hurry to get up. Maureen hurried to him, bent over him.

'Jim, oh, Jim! Are you hurt...?'

Her brother swore at her and pushed her away from him. The girl came erect, her eyes twin barbs directed at the visitor. Webb paid no heed. He was striding across to the mounted men.

'You boys his pards?'

Neither of them answered him.

'Damn it, can't you hear me? If you're his friends, say so and come and back him up. Or could it be that you're both yellow?'

The taller of the pair poked at his stubbled cheek while he writhed under the cowman's contempt. He dropped to the ground finally, circled Webb experimentally.

A hard voice rapped from the veranda. 'Don't make a move. That means nobody.'

Josh Parker had his Peacemaker levelled and was moving it in a slow, sweeping arc. Webb spat in disgust, put his back to Parker, and went to his sorrel. He was in leather by the time Jim had managed to clamber to his feet.

'Don't come back,' he mouthed. 'Drift on out of here or you'll regret it.'

Webb nudged his horse forward. He glimpsed the girl back on the veranda, hands clutching the rails, watching him. But he paid no heed and continued out of the yard, making for the cottonwoods and willows along the creek.

When he reached the spot where the girl had been washing her dress he halted to peer over his shoulder. There was no sign of Jim. His two companions were staring after him, saying something to each other. He saw Maureen at the far end of the veranda, where she had shifted to watch his departure. Even as he watched, she hurried into the house.

Webb followed the course of the creek until he reached the point where the timber banked greenly against the reddening sky. Here he halted again and brought makings from his shirt pocket. He touched his bruised lips gingerly, grinning in a wry fashion. His knuckles tingled, and his shoulder and arm muscles sang pleasantly. The cigarette burning to his satisfaction, he pushed his sorrel on into the timber.

When they could no longer see him, the two arrivals who had accompanied Jim to the Silver Creek homestead squatted beside the porch and smoked morosely, until Jim emerged from the house. He was accompanied by his sister and father, and it was evident that there had been a difficult altercation, as the girl's cheeks were flushed.

'If you start fighting with everybody who comes along you won't last long,' she warned her brother in a belated shot.

'Ah, take your spurs off, Reen,' the other retorted sulkily. 'I'll run into that *hombre* again some time. And when I do...' He left the rest hanging ominously, but his father simply shook his head and spat in the dust.

'Struck me as a pretty nice jasper,' Parker commented. 'One thing's for sure: he could use his fists like a prize-fighter!'

The pair down in the yard had straightened, and the taller one observed: 'Fighting was a mistake right enough, Jim. You could have run into a dozen cowmen and it wouldn't have mattered. But that one...' He shook his head gravely.

The girl stared at the speaker, but it was left to her brother to demand an explanation. 'What the devil are you driving at, Single?' he rasped.

'You saying you don't know who that gent is?'

'Say, what is this? I don't know him and I don't give a curse who he is.' Still, it was evident that he was concerned all the same.

'He's Webb Bannister,' Single revealed. 'Owner of the Triangle B outfit to the north of here.'

Maureen Parker's hand leaped to her mouth and she stared along the creek to the spot where she had last seen the visitor. He was gone, of course. All she saw were the trees shimmering in the fading light.

'Oh, no!' she whispered. 'Not him! Then we're ruined before we've even got properly started...'

TWO

Webb did not head home directly. He knew he would run into Pete Hogan and would be obliged to explain about Silver Creek. What would he say? Perhaps he could tell his foreman that he had bypassed the creek and would pay a visit to the squatters another time. But that wouldn't work. Pete was against the dirt-farmers, not solely on account of their turning over grass roots and running chickens and hogs, but because of their proclivities for thieving. Pete maintained they were a form of range rot that could be cured only by cutting it out.

Webb's thoughts lingered on the girl, Maureen. A nice name that, a nice girl if you confined your judgment to looks. For the rest – temperament, behaviour and inclination – she was a positive wildcat, ready to jump at a man for looking at her. He touched his mouth again. It still bled a little. Anyhow, he had shown Jim what was what. Jim was a dangerous character, brash and cocky, and it looked as if he was mixing with bad company.

Webb could not place the riders whom Jim had brought to the homestead. Something about the taller of the pair was vaguely familiar, and he must have seen him before somewhere. But their brand was obvious – riff-raff, the type of coyotes that skulked about the range with their noses eternally sniffing out easy pickings.

Were his cattle supposed to be the pickings in this instance? Yes, that could well be the case. He wondered if either of the pair had recognized him; he didn't think so, however.

He might not have had the chance to ride away like that had they known who he was.

The thought jarred him. He decided he had been a fool for not making his errand known at the very outset. There was only one way to handle that stripe – roughly, without gloves: tell them to clear off, and keep a gun trained on them until they complied.

The sun was dropping below the horizon by then. Streamers of rosy fire stretched across the west, fading into weaker tints; they made a last stand against the encroaching darkness. The air was cooler. The tang of the timber lost its sharpness; a dampness lifted from the earth. Wreaths of mist swirled ghostily in the hollows, swallowing thickets, boulders. Webb changed his mind about avoiding Pete Hogan and picked up the trail for home when he broke out of the trees.

The big rambling ranch-house had lost something of its sparkle and driving force on the death of the Old Man. Webb's father had risen too early from a sick-bed after an attack of pneumonia and fallen dead from his horse, and for Pete Hogan it had been the end of an era. The foreman had averred privately that it would be the finish, too, of Triangle B. Young Webb, with his newfangled ideas gathered with a tenderfoot education in Chicago, his easy-going ways, and his leniency with cattle thieves and other range parasites, would soon swamp out the fire the Old Man had kindled and kept going with his labour and his sweat.

After six months, Pete Hogan had seen no reason to change his opinion.

Arriving at headquarters, Webb gave his sorrel to the stable-hand and learned that Pete was looking for him. In the house, Webb washed and donned a clean shirt. He was surveying his bruised lips in the wall mirror in the living-room when the front door thundered and Hogan's voice bellowed through the place.

'You in there, Boss?'

'Come ahead.'

Webb silently cursed the man. Pete had never asked the Old Man's permission to enter the house, but had barged in at will, when the mood took him, without preamble of any sort. This mock courtesy was something that caused Webb's blood to boil.

He lowered the wick of the lamp a trifle so that his injury might not be easily observed, and was poking a cigar out of a box when the foreman entered. Hogan stood in the middle of the room, a small man, wide of shoulder and narrow of hip, with stocky legs that resembled powerful tree-trunks, and too-long arms that gave him a curious, ape-like appearance. His face was squarely-hewn and brown as coffee; his eyes were hard chips of light, and just then were coloured with expectancy.

'You didn't eat supper,' he accused.

'Didn't feel hungry, Pete. Sit down, light your pipe if you want to.' Webb sank into an easy chair as he spoke. Pete Hogan stared at him.

'Who hit you?' he demanded bluntly.

'Huh?' Webb contrived to look surprised. The bright eyes grew beady, suspicious.

'Somebody busted your lip,' Pete said. 'Did you have trouble with the Parkers?'

'I didn't think you knew them,' Webb countered, flailing himself for the defensive attitude he was adopting.

'Not much,' Hogan grunted. He sat down opposite, brought out his pipe and tobacco pouch. 'There's a gal as well,' he proclaimed sententiously.

'You didn't tell me that.'

'I offered to ride down with you. I know them. Did that Jim fella get smart with his fists?'

Webb levered himself out of the chair,

paced the room. He sighed and turned up the lamp-light, batting at the flies buzzing in the yellow flare. He nodded.

'Yeah, we had a difference of opinion.'

'You said "yeah" there,' Hogan sneered mildly. 'And I heard you saying "ain't" the other day. Better watch all that book-learning don't get rubbed away. Did Jim Jasper really paste you?'

Webb resolved to keep his temper. 'Why didn't you tell me you knew something about the family, Pete? You knew I was green about them.'

'Green,' Hogan murmured. He sighed, paying no heed to Webb's barbed glare. 'Do you know what the Old Man would have done with that crowd?'

'Sure, I know,' Webb growled. 'He'd have taken the whole outfit to the creek, armed to the teeth. He might have burned them out if they refused to leave.'

Hogan said softly: 'You're saying they're still there? You didn't give them their marching orders?'

'Quit riding me, Pete. Some times I think you forget that I'm the boss of Triangle B now.'

The foreman lifted his shoulder in a fine display of resignation. 'All right, boy. Sing your song if you like. Where does it get you? That damned Parker slapped you in the kisser and told you where to go, didn't he? I know him, Webb; I know his kind. You should have let me go with you. I can handle that breed...'

'Shut up, damn it.'

Hogan rose. 'Anything you say, Boss. As you just pointed out: you're the fella that gives the orders and we're the jaspers that do what we're told. Say, you know something? You can fire me if you like. Now, I reckon that's about the best way of getting me off'n your back.'

'So long, Pete. I'm going to be sick in a minute.'

'Make sure you get something to cure your lip,' was the cryptic response.

Hogan went on out and Webb listened to his boots clumping over the porch, down the steps. His spur rowels jingled. Pete was on his way to the bunkhouse for his nightly game of poker. Sometimes Webb joined in, but he had to make the effort. The men were so damnably polite with him. They treated him as they might treat some stranger they had been warned to handle carefully. They were deferential, of course. They laid that on really thick. They could call him Mr

Bannister without batting an eyelid.

The Old Man had always been the Old Man with them. When they disagreed with his views or his actions they soon let him know. When he tramped on their toes they would swear in his face. When that happened, the Old Man used to laugh gleefully, confident in the knowledge that they were his kind and he would never have to travel beyond their reach to find a friend.

His son had been in saddle for six months now, but he was still the stranger, the unknown quantity whom nobody cared to let into their circle. Pete Hogan knew all this, and sure as the devil, Pete had never done anything to remedy the situation. If anything, he gave free rein to his tart tongue in the presence of the crew, so that Webb had been forced to swallow a poison brew on more than one occasion.

He might have fired Pete, but even if he did give this angle serious consideration, he knew there would be a real danger of most of the crew quitting along with the foreman.

Now Hogan had been given another needle to jab into him – the run-in with the Parkers at Silver Creek and his abject failure where getting rid of the nesters was concerned. It was characteristic of the foreman that he had not withheld judgment until he had heard a full explanation. He had simply concluded that Jim Parker had licked the hell out of him and sent him home with his tail down.

Webb could have given him the true side of the story, of course, and he might have done so had the foreman behaved in a civil manner. But again, Hogan might greet the truth with scepticism. Anyhow, Webb told himself that he didn't give a tinker's curse about the foreman's opinion, or the opinion of the men in the bunkhouse, for that matter.

He went outside to the coolness of the night shortly, puffing at another cigar, and squatted on the top step of the veranda. A breeze riffled the dust in the yard and blew in the scent of grass and sage. He could hear some shouting from the bunkhouse, the whinnying of horses in the corral beyond. Another sound contrived a backdrop for these safe and familiar noises – the low drumming of hoofbeats angling in from the open range.

Webb faced the direction of the newcomer's approach, threw his cigar stub away when the rider slowed, then shifted about in a half circle as though undecided about something. Webb was on his feet when the new arrival put his horse through the gateway, steam lifting from its body in small clouds. He watched the man curiously for another moment, then said: 'You're at Triangle B if you don't know.'

The man who dismounted was of average height, slim of build. He draped the reins over the head of his mount and approached until the meagre light from the window behind Webb fell on his face.

He was aware of a little shock on realizing this was one of the men he had encountered at the Silver Creek homestead.

'I want to speak to the boss.' The voice was low-pitched, gusty. The man had ridden a long way by the looks of him and his steaming horse.

'You're looking at him,' Webb informed him.

'Webb Banister! Say, where can we talk, Mr Bannister?'

'What's wrong with right here?'

'This could be mighty important to you, Bannister. You saw me at the Parker place today, with Singleton McCall...'

'I remember. You had no stomach for fighting. Your pard would have joined the party, though.'

'A man needs a cause to fight for,' was the

34

terse response. 'I heard a fella who knew a thing or two say that one time. Man who picks a fight over nothing is worse than a fool.'

'You're no fool then?'

'I've been around for quite a spell.'

'That figures. Look ... come on inside.'

He led the way back into the house and through to the big, comfortable living-room. He nodded the newcomer to a chair, but he was nervous about something, jumpy. He stood and worked his greasy hat through his fingers.

'This is a sort of deal, Mr Bannister.'

That figured as well. Webb could smell a nest of rats, but he forced himself to incline his head and smile encouragingly. He kept watching those dark, close-set eyes. The face as a whole reminded him of a fox without that animal's clean, natural wholesomeness.

'What's your name, friend?'

'That doesn't matter.'

'It might, you know. If there's a deal in the air we'll need to know exactly where we stand, including each other's name. You already have the advantage.'

'I'm Mal Jordan,' was the grudging response.

'That's better.' Webb fished in his pocket

for the makings. He stood on the opposite side of the big table and rolled his smoke. 'What's your deal?' He was highly suspicious of the whole set-up. Jim Parker could have sent Jordan here on some pretext to further his grudge against the Triangle B. Webb had a notion that by this time Parker would know the identity of his opponent. How might the father have reacted? And the girl, Maureen?

'I know of a big rustle being planned on your stock,' Jordan told him in an excited rush. He paused and ran his tongue across his underlip. 'I thought you might be interested.'

Webb frowned. Instead of agreeing that, naturally, he was interested, he said: 'I see. Would the Parkers be mixed up in this?'

'That's all part of the deal, mister. When we clinch it.'

Webb bit down an angry retort. He had an urge to grab this weasel by the neck and shake him until his teeth rattled in his head and he spilled everything he knew. Jordan divined his thoughts.

'I don't have to talk if I don't want to,' he warned. 'I'm an honest man, and nobody's got anything against me.'

Webb's nostrils dilated. 'How much?' he asked bluntly.

'Couple of hundred.'

Webb exploded in a laugh which he deliberately made harsh. 'You're here to peddle information my men can bring to me for nothing? What kind of fool do you take me for, Jordan?'

'Your boys don't have this information.' Jordan rubbed his nose and backed slowly to the doorway.

'Wait! How would I know if your information is worth the breath you use?'

'When you hear it I reckon you'll know all right.'

Webb sighed. He had a choice here. He could hold Jordan and fetch Pete and a couple of the boys. They could lock this man up until he talked, or take him to Yellow Fork and hand him over to the sheriff there. Or he could pay Jordan his two hundred dollars and hear what he had to say.

It didn't take him long to reach a decision. 'I'm sorry, mister. I don't like the sound of your deal. I can't say that I'm taken with you much, either. I reckon Triangle B can take care of its own problems.'

The newcomer was sweating a little now. It was evident that he had banked a lot on the Triangle B boss seeing things his way and buying his information. Disappoint-

37

ment made his face even leaner than it was; the eyes appeared to get smaller.

'I just figured I was doing you a favour, mister.'

'And doing yourself a favour as well.'

'You might regret not taking up my offer,' Jordan said surlily.

Webb took a quick step towards him, restrained himself. He made a gesture of dismissal. 'Get going, friend, before some of the boys find out you're here and what you're about.'

Jordan went to his horse and clambered aboard. He said in a different tone: 'So it's true after all what they say about the new Triangle B boss?'

'What have *you* got to say about it?' Webb rasped.

'They say you're going to stand back and let the whole works fall in pieces around you. So long, Mr Bannister.'

Webb glared after him, listened to the sound of his mount's hooves cutting away out through the grass. His jaw slumped; his breath hissed through his teeth. He went into the house and retrieved his gun-belt, buckled it on. Then he brought the stableman to the corral and had him saddle up a sturdy chestnut. The man made no comment, just worked quickly and efficiently. He handed the reins to his boss with a smile.

'Thanks, Jed. If Pete happens to be looking for me, tell him I won't be long.'

'Sure thing, Mr Bannister.'

Webb took the chestnut across the gloom-cloaked yard, mounted when he was beyond the gateway, and set off into the night. It might be worthwhile following Mal Jordan, but he had no idea where the rider was headed. Still, if Jordan had got wind of a big rustling move there was only one place he could have heard it – at Silver Creek.

He went over the trail he had taken earlier, angling towards the woods that loomed against the star-shot heavens. He had travelled about four miles from headquarters when he heard a shot. The explosion rippled out of the stillness ahead of him, and he dragged down on his reins, peering into the murk.

There was nothing to be seen. The explosion had sounded like the bark of a revolver. He turned his head to listen but heard nothing more. After some minutes he pressed his horse into motion, making for the point where he judged the shot had been fired. He soon reached the fringe of trees and rode about for a while, in a slow, tightening circle. He moved warily, with his hand on his gun butt.

The chestnut gave him the first hint of warning. It had drawn level with a jumble of rocks when it halted suddenly and whickered. Webb patted the beast's neck and slid to the earth, bringing his Colt clear. There was little light just then, but he soon made out a shape on the ground. He raised his revolver.

'Who is it?'

No answer. Behind him, the chestnut was making more commotion. It trotted off a short distance, wheeled, and came back. Webb looked around him carefully. He let a long minute drag by, then approached the form lying in the shadows. A premonition took hold of him and grew, and even before he stooped over the outstretched man he could have told who he was. It was the rider who had introduced himself as Mal Jordan, who had offered to sell him information. He lay at a grotesque angle, legs doubled beneath him. Both hands were outstretched, and in one of them a revolver was clutched.

Webb worked the gun out of his fingers and sniffed the barrel. It hadn't been Jordan's gun he had heard going off. Which meant there was a killer lurking out there somewhere in the darkness.

The chestnut was thoroughly nervous by this time and began edging away. Nevertheless, Webb took the time it required to circle the jumble of boulders and work his way back to the horse. There was no trace of the horse that Jordan would have ridden, no clue to the killer's whereabouts. Exactly what had happened here? Had Jordan argued with his friend or friends? Had he threatened to spill the beans unless they did things the way he decided?

It was easy enough guessing at a motive, but how could he be sure he was right? Even so, he was pretty certain that the killing was tied in with a proposed rustling raid on his stock. He should have sent for Pete Hogan on Jordan's arrival at headquarters, should have asked Pete's advice instead of taking things into his own hands. Was it too late to return to the ranch and dig out Pete and some of the boys?

He mounted and cut on towards the timber. A wafer of moon was trying to clear a cloud-pack. Instead of riding into the woods as he had done on his earlier visit to Silver Creek he made a detour that took him over rougher country. A coyote yapped from an elevation on his left. He smiled grimly, wondering what Pete's reaction would be if he knew of his mission.

Finally, he was close to the creek, but about half a mile away from the homestead site. He slowed his pace when he hit the watercourse. The creek had appeared to run silently by daylight; now he could hear the whisper and tinkle and gurgle of the water.

When he was about a quarter-mile from the ramshackle buildings he took the chestnut into a grove of willows and tied it securely to a stout branch. The horse was proving to be a more nervous beast than the sorrel, and he didn't want to risk being seen until he was able to make an unhindered surveillance of the homestead site.

He hugged the cottonwoods and willows all the way, and was at the spot where he had come on the girl washing her dress when he drew up abruptly. Someone was sitting on a rock close to the edge of the water.

Webb had his revolver levelled when the figure lunged erect, poised in preparation for flight.

'Don't move!' Webb barked.

The figure froze and he shifted on down the bank, at the same time dividing his attention so that he could watch the whole area. When he drew much closer he halted and drew a ragged breath.

'Maureen!'

The figure came at him like a tigress, heedless of the gun in his fingers, hitting out wildly with her small fists. Webb was forced to retreat, pushing his revolver into its holster. Then he was obliged to come to grips with her, hearing her laboured breathing and short, choked-off sobs. Her nails clawed at his face before he had her arms held tight at her sides. Even then, she kicked at his legs and ankles.

'If you don't quit, I'll lay you out cold,' he hissed furiously.

She went lax at that, her bosom rising and falling rapidly. She was sobbing uncontrollably now. Webb released her and stood back.

'Miss Parker – Maureen – what on earth's the matter? Did I frighten you coming up the way I did?'

'What do you want here?' she demanded hoarsely. 'Can't you leave us alone? We might be living on the edge of your land, but we're not causing any harm.'

Webb let a few seconds go past without speaking, waiting until she had regained some semblance of composure. Then he said: 'Is your brother at home?'

'I don't know. What does it matter? It's none of your business anyway.'

'You could be wrong,' he reasoned. 'Listen and I'll tell you what happened tonight.' He continued quickly as she showed signs of getting ready to flee: 'I had a visit from one of the men who were with your brother today. Name of Mal Jordan.'

'I don't know him. I don't know who they were. I don't want to hear anything about them.'

'I'm sorry, Maureen, but you'd better hear, I guess. Jordan told me he had information to sell about a proposed cattle raid on my range. I refused to do a deal with him. When he left my place I rode out behind him. I was trying to track him when I heard a shot. When I came on Jordan he was dead.'

'Then – then you killed him.'

'Of course I didn't,' Webb snapped impatiently. 'But somebody killed him. Has anyone called at your home during the last hour or so?'

She shook her head. It was hard to believe that this was the same high-spirited girl he had encountered earlier in the evening. He was about to ask her if her brother was at home when she suddenly sidestepped him, whirled about, and sped away into the shadows.

THREE

Webb was trapped in indecision. His first impulse was to go after the girl, tell her that he meant no harm to her, but he checked it. How was he to know how things were shaping and what fate would dictate? He tried to guess what Maureen's reactions to their second meeting would be, wondered if Jim was at home with his father and the rider called Singleton McCall. He wondered if it was they who were planning the rustling foray on Triangle B stock: was it they who had killed Mal Jordan when he left the Bannister headquarters?

After a few minutes he went back to his horse. He broke the reins loose and crossed the creek, then worked his way towards the homestead from the rear. When the outlines of the main building hove into view he settled down to wait and watch. It was a risky business, he knew, but he simply had to find out some answers.

Time passed and nothing happened. There was no light in the back of the house, no sign of life at all. Tiring of his vigil at length, he caught the chestnut's reins and completed the circle, finishing up where he could watch the front of the house.

There was light at this side, at least, even if it glowed from only one window. It was difficult to distinguish shape or form in the darkness, but there was no saddle-stock in evidence that he could see. He began to have the feeling that he was wasting time. Had Jim been at home, the girl would have roused him out long ago, telling her brother that Webb Bannister had come back to skulk around and spy on them. Jim would be only too pleased at the excuse to hit back at Bannister.

He was about to leave the chestnut again and move in closer to the house when a rustling at his back caused him to swivel sharply.

'A bad move and you're dead, mister,' he was warned.

Webb's fingers had reached the butt of his revolver, but he checked the action, glimpsing the figure of a man, and seeing the weapon he held levelled.

'Josh Parker!'

'Pity you got that itch to slip around in the dark, young fella,' Parker said bleakly. 'You know where we live,' he added with a touch of sourness. 'Get to walking over there, and mind your manners.'

Webb started to reach for his horse, but a growl told him to let the animal be. 'Ain't that far to walk. Go ahead now.'

Webb flailed himself for a fool as he preceded the old-timer to the veranda. Just as he reached the three rickety steps the girl appeared, a rifle tucked in at her side and the muzzle trained on him.

Webb gulped. 'Seems everybody's out hunting tonight.'

'Yep,' Parker grunted. 'Including you, mister.'

'Now, you'd better listen to me,' Webb exploded. 'You've no right to hold me up like this. Do you happen to know who I am?'

'Oh, I happen to know that all right,' Parker drawled. There was no trace now of the ingenuous, easy-going dirt farmer. This man was alert and wary, and Webb had no doubt about him being perfectly capable of squeezing the trigger of his revolver and pumping a bullet into him. 'But it don't matter a damn who you are,' Parker added. 'Especially when you're caught snooping on honest folks in the dark.'

A vicious pressure against his ribs made

Webb mount the steps. The girl moved aside wordlessly as her father pushed the unwelcome caller into the house. When they reached the small living-room, Webb looked around him. Jim was not here, or if he was at home he intended keeping out of sight. Webb was pressed against the far wall, and Parker relieved him of his Colt in a deft, seemingly practiced, action. Then he stepped back out of range.

'All right, Mr Bannister, you can sit down. Over there.' He indicated a straight-backed chair and Webb shifted to it under the watchful eye of the girl.

There was no sign of tears now, and her eyes held a hardness that took his breath away. What if this whole family were involved in large-scale rustling and would take whatever steps were necessary to protect or conceal their activities?

Josh Parker moved to the edge of the table and perched there. His brows were knotted in what appeared to be furious thought. The hand that held the revolver was rock-steady and fuelled Webb's consternation.

The girl placed her rifle against the wall. She appeared strangely, almost unnaturally, calm. She gave Webb the impression that she was holding her fears and her impulses in check. He forced a tight grin.

'Sure is a cosy party, isn't it? Only, I can't say that I'm entirely comfortable.' He glanced meaningly at the revolver Parker was holding on him.

Parker cleared his throat. He appeared somewhat self-conscious at this juncture. 'What do you want down here, Mr Bannister?'

Webb started at the use of the courtesy title. His grin became crooked. 'I'd rather you just called me Bannister. Or Webb.'

Parker was having none of his levity. His mouth tightened and his eyes narrowed. 'I'm waiting for an answer, fella. Rancher or not, it don't give you any right to stick your nose into folks' private affairs.'

'Did your daughter tell you about the man I found dead?'

'A good yarn. But lies won't get you nowhere. Why don't you just admit you're trying to be tricky, Mr Bannister?'

'It's the truth, nevertheless. That Mal Jordan who was here with your son and the one called Single or Singleton... Jordan came to my place tonight and tried to make a deal with me. He said he had information about a plan to steal my cattle. He wanted me to give him two hundred dollars for details of the supposed raid.'

'What did he tell you?' Parker sounded sceptical, puzzled.

'He told me nothing. He had no intention of talking without getting paid for it. I'd no intention of paying him anything.'

'What happened then? He just leave your place?'

'That's what he did. I took a horse out with the idea of following him. I lost him, but I kept going towards the timber. Then I heard a shot, and after looking around for a while I found Jordan. As I've told you, he was dead.'

'So maybe you killed him yourself, huh? Maybe you got kind of scared out in the woods? When a fella's scared in the dark he's liable to get an itchy trigger finger.'

Webb's mouth hardened with anger. He tried to curb his feelings. 'That's what I believe your daughter thought,' he said patiently. 'But I didn't kill him. You can check my gun if you like. No, Parker, somebody else killed Mal Jordan. Don't you see,' he went on in a different tone while his gaze switched to the girl, 'this could be serious for you. Serious for your daughter, your son, Jim.'

Maureen felt compelled to comment at this stage. 'Since when did the owner of a ranch like the Triangle B worry about a family of farmers?' she demanded scornfully. 'We know how your men work, Mr Bannister. They ride out at night and order people from their homes at gunpoint.'

Webb drew a hard, steadying breath. This kind of talk always made him see red. 'They used to,' he conceded patiently. 'Maybe when my father was alive. You've been listening to stories...'

Josh Parker was leaning forward hopefully as he talked. 'Am I to take it that you don't intend to kick us off this land?'

Webb hesitated, squirmed under the burning eyes that drilled into him. What could he say – give a promise to these people that they wouldn't be bothered with his men, with Pete Hogan? He could almost see Pete standing back in the shadows, listening to him; could almost hear his mocking laughter.

'See!' the girl erupted passionately. 'He's trying to bluff us, Dad. He's just like the rest of the cattlemen we've run up against. They think they're the lords of the earth, superbeings who treat homesteaders like dirt. They'll never change their ideas or their ways.'

'It's not how it is at all,' Webb protested. 'You don't seem to understand–'

51

'All right,' Parker grunted. 'So we don't understand. So you make us understand, Mr Bannister. I still think you're bluffing, but I guess you'd better make your play anyhow.'

'Put yourself in my place,' Webb reasoned. 'I'm trying to run a cattle outfit. I'm losing more stock than I can afford to lose.'

'Ah!' Parker snarled. 'So now you're calling us thieves? This is getting more like the truth.'

Webb was fast losing patience with both of them. They might be innocent enough; they might simply be trying to put down roots in a place they liked. On the other hand, they could be playing a deep game of bluff themselves.

He decided to put the whole business to the test.

'Where's your son, Josh?'

'Jim? How should I know? He's a man, ain't he? None of your business anyhow, Mr Bannister. So long as he ain't–'

'Stealing my cattle,' Webb suggested coldly when he broke off.

'Damn you,' the other cried. 'I've a good mind to let this trigger go.'

'Let it go,' Webb taunted. 'Go ahead and get a hemp necktie fitted around your neck.' His fury knew no bounds just then. He gauged the distance separating him from Parker. A mere yard. Dare he risk it?

He acted even as the thought formed. He heard the girl give a shriek, and knew she would make a grab for the rifle. His closed fist smote the back of the homesteader's hand and the revolver clattered to the floor. Parker bellowed and went after it. Webb stamped hard on his fingers, then swung on the girl. She was bringing the rifle up when he crashed into her and sent her spinning with the sheer weight and force of his body.

They scrambled for the rifle together. Webb reached for it first and flung the weapon through the doorway. He heard it connect with something before it clattered to the ground. Parker had grasped his revolver again when Webb caught him a neat clip to the angle of his jaw and sent him floundering into a corner, where his head struck the wall. Webb reached down for the revolver and stuck it under his belt.

He should have been ready for the girl launching herself at him.

This time he was in no mood for niceties. He simply blocked her initial rush solidly and heaved her against the maple dresser. Her pliant form lunged against him, soft and warm behind the strength she exerted.

Then he had her arms pinned to her sides.

'You damned wildcat...'

'I'll kill you,' she threatened furiously.

'Not this time, Maureen.' His voice thickened and some of the fire went out of the girl's eyes. For an instant there was fear, the dawning of some other emotion. Webb released her abruptly and stepped back. Parker was trying to get to his feet. He ranted and swore, breathless, the veins in his forehead corded.

A crisp comment issued from the doorway.

'Well, if this ain't a touching scene!'

Webb spun, fingers falling to his holstered Colt. The action froze as he found himself looking into the dark face and glittering eyes of Pete Hogan.

For the space of five seconds a tense silence held the room; it was broken by Josh Parker hustling for a breath. Then the girl emitted a little yelp of alarm and Pete Hogan's lips curled in disdain.

'So you finally found a situation you could handle, Boss, eh?'

Webb could have killed his foreman where he stood. Josh Parker sank down on a chair and patted the sweat from his forehead with a bandana handkerchief. He muttered something under his breath. Maureen had sidled to the door and was in the act of slipping out.

'Come back here, damn you,' Hogan snarled. 'You ain't dealing with a lapdog now.'

Maureen moved away from him, real fear shining in her eyes. Her father appeared to have surrendered to what he believed to be the inevitable. Both of them knew Pete Hogan, and were familiar with the cowman's methods. Webb saw a grim, detestable significance in the meek way they were capitulating.

'So you followed me?' he accused his foreman.

Hogan smiled without warmth. His gaze embraced the three of them, sought warily for others who might be lurking somewhere out of sight. He dipped his head.

'That's right, I did. Wonder what'll happen to you when you run out of wet nurses.'

Webb coloured. He felt the weight of the girl's stare on him, assessing him afresh, watching his reactions with avid interest in spite of her own plight.

'Anyone else at home who'd like to join the fun?' Pete wanted to know.

'Nobody,' Webb said curtly.

'Well, maybe you're beginning to learn, at that, Boss. Good idea of yours to come back here when the boy ain't at home.'

'Don't you worry none,' Parker snapped, recovering some of his nerve. 'My boy ain't scared of your boss. He ain't hiding. He'll set tight till he gets his own back.'

'His own back?' Hogan's brows arched. He frowned at Webb. 'How come? What's he driving at?'

'Forget it, Pete.'

'Say, you ain't telling me you really beat that Jim fella?' Hogan queried with a broken laugh.

He sobered as the girl addressed him, her words hitting the foreman like small pellets of ice. 'He picked a fight with my brother,' she said. 'Knocked him down. That's what father means. Jim won't forget it in a hurry.'

'Hell, I bet he won't!' Hogan regarded the man who employed him, and who could send him packing if he chose to say the word. 'Well, well, so you're a dark horse after all!'

'I told you to forget it, Pete.'

'Anything you say, Boss.' Hogan became brisk. 'All right, folks. I want to tell you that my heart ain't made of stone like you figure, but I've got a job to do all the same. I spotted a wagon round back. The boss and me will help you harness a team and get loaded up.'

Parker and his daughter exchanged looks. Hot resentment glittered in the regard the girl put on Webb Bannister. Her father inclined his head in response to her unspoken challenge.

'No sense in arguing, honey,' he said fatalistically. 'No sense in fighting neither. This place is just like all the others we stopped at. Owned by cowmen. Guarded by trigger-itchy *hombres* like Bannister's foreman here. Likely he's got a bunch of his men around the house at this minute.'

'Wouldn't matter one way or the other, Parker,' Pete Hogan commented while he plucked at the lobe of his right ear. He kept his eyes averted from Webb. 'This is Triangle B territory, and it's going to stay that way.'

'But we've fixed this place up,' the girl protested with a little groan. 'Spent money on it, time. Made the house fit to live in...'

'I grant that you've done a pretty good job, ma'am. All the same—'

'Take it easy, Pete,' Webb interjected. 'It appears to me that you're overlooking one very important point.'

'Huh?' The cowman's eyes drilled into his own, suspicious, shaded with a terrible intuition. 'Say, you're not going to tell me you're backing these people?' he retorted disbelievingly.

'Call it whatever you like,' was Webb's gruff rejoinder. 'We can't just tell them to pack their wagon and drift. It would be less than fair. No, Pete, I intend to let them stay, for the time being anyhow.'

Hogan appeared mesmerised for a few moments. It seemed that he had lost the ability to breathe, to comprehend. And when the full horror of what was happening dawned on him, he said thickly: 'You're crazy, Webb. You know that, don't you? Why, you're turning every rule on its head, every belief that cowmen live by. And I'll tell you something else,' he went on with the suggestion of foam flecking the sides of his mouth. 'You'll end up being the laughing-stock of this range.'

'That's as maybe.' Webb tried to sound amenable. 'But I think I know what I'm doing.'

'Say!' the foreman cried on a high note when he caught Webb glancing at the girl. 'I believe I'm beginning to see light. Parker's daughter, by grab! You've let a pretty female turn your head...'

'Easy now, Pete.'

'Easy hell, boy. It's the truth, and you can't

deny it. Just wait till the boys hear about this!' Hogan spun on his heel in disgust and headed for the doorway. Webb caught his sleeve and brought him around.

'I'm telling you to go easy, Pete.'

'Want me to quit?' the other growled ominously.

'Quit and be hanged,' Webb snapped. 'I'm sick of listening to your bellyaching about one thing or other.'

'You might find yourself without any outfit, boy. Don't say I didn't warn you.'

Webb's chest heaved under the pressure. With an effort he controlled the raw anger swirling in him. 'You must suit yourself,' he said at length.

The foreman went out at that. A few moments later they heard a horse stamping in the yard, then a ragged, rebellious shout and the hammering of hooves as Pete Hogan pulled out.

There was another long silence when he had gone. Josh Parker sat like a man bemused, scarcely daring to believe what he had seen and heard. Finally, he shook his head, grinned crookedly.

'You're getting yourself into a heap of trouble on account of us, Mr Bannister. You don't have to.'

'I'm old enough to make my own decisions.'

The girl took a step towards him, halted with dark colour sweeping through her cheeks. She went on through to her bedroom without speaking and Webb went outside, leaving Parker staring after him.

Webb breathed deeply of the night air. He could catch the tattoo of Pete's horse angling towards the south. Where was Pete making for, he wondered. Well, it didn't really matter much now. The cards were down and it remained to be seen who would scoop the pot.

He went over to the chestnut and levered himself to the saddle. He checked an impulse to go into wild flight. Why should he? He had as much right to be on this land as anybody; more right, when it came to the crunch. He took the time it required to finger out the makings and roll himself a cigarette. He scratched a match to life, casting a glance at the front door of the house. It stood open, making a triangle of dim yellow light. But no one emerged. Everything was silent, almost eerily so. He nudged his horse into motion, forded the creek, and took the trail Pete Hogan had taken. He was possessed with a gnawing curiosity to know where Pete was going.

At the end of a half-hour or so he glimpsed a figure up in front of him, on the crest of a ridge that fell away into a section of rocks and scrub. A nervous tingle traced its way along his spine and he palmed his revolver. If Hogan didn't know it, Webb Bannister was as proficient with a shot-gun or rifle as he was with his fists. He moved in closer and knew beyond doubt that the horseman was Pete.

The foreman's face was a pale blob in the darkness; the eyes glinted in a mischievous grin.

'Reckoned somehow you'd come after me.' His laugh was shaky.

'You reckon a whole lot, pard,' Webb observed in a conversational manner. 'You think Triangle B couldn't do without you.' He was in no mood for double talk, or humour with a fork in its tail. 'Are you heading off without collecting your pay?'

'Listen to me, Webb.' Hogan sounded perfectly serious. 'When I plan to quit the outfit I'll tell you. I hope you're not going to kick me off before I'm ready to go.'

'Last thing on my mind. Anyhow, I'm not very good at kicking folks around.'

'You might learn how to do it properly one of these days,' was the wry rejoinder. 'And now,' Hogan went on with his customary brashness, 'what happened to the gent that paid the call on you?'

Webb was glad of the darkness to conceal his surprise. 'You long-eared fox! I thought nobody saw him arriving at the ranch, or leaving, for that matter.'

'Like blazes!' Hogan said forcefully. 'What do you think we are – a lot of kids waiting for the wolf to come and gobble us up? I saw him all right, and I watched him slope off again. I heard a little of what he said to you... All right, all right! So I've got long ears. But I'm paid for having long ears. I'm paid for eavesdropping, if needs be. Didn't you try to trail him?'

This further evidence of Pete's alertness and interest in the workings of the ranch had the effect of taking the wind out of Webb's sails to some degree.

'Do you believe some gang really is planning to help themselves to our cattle?' he countered carefully.

'Hard to say.' Hogan brought his pipe out, thumbed the dottle down in the bowl, and struck a match to puff it alight. 'Maybe that geezer just took you for an easy touch. Two hundred dollars! Now that's what I call taking a man for a real trip through the cactus!

If I'd been you, I'd have booted him off the ranch instead of letting him ride off.'

Webb sprang his own surprise in a low-pitched voice. 'He won't ride anywhere any more. He's dead. That was his name – Mal Jordan.'

'What! Damn it, that shot I heard... Did you–'

'Not me, Pete: somebody else. I hunted around after I heard the shot and found Jordan. He was already dead.'

'But the killer...'

'I searched for him. Not a trace.'

Hogan blew gustily through his teeth. He puffed at his pipe for a minute, cast a look along the trail that led to Silver Creek. 'Now, look, Webb, you think I was hard on that Parker family. But you'll have to get it into your head that all these hoemen have the makings of rustlers. It's what makes them such a damn nuisance. Would you keep a coyote in your chicken-run? And that Jim fella wasn't there, remember. He's too damn slick and sly for my liking.'

Webb nodded soberly. 'I think he might be up to something, Pete. He and that one they call Singleton.'

'McCall?' Hogan almost howled. 'Well, that's a dirty crook if ever there was one.

Did you see Single?'

'He was at the Parker homestead earlier with Mal Jordan and Jim. It's what makes me figure there could be something serious in the wind. Otherwise, why kill Jordan for talking to me?'

'For offering to squeal, you mean. Now, let's do some calculating. Nearest Triangle B stuff to Silver Creek is over at Apache Basin. I've got two of the boys nighthawking over there, Sloan and Cartwright. But here, you never can tell...'

'Let's take a look,' Webb suggested. 'It's only a few miles from where we are now.'

'Why didn't I bring some of the boys along with me,' Hogan fretted. 'Come on then.'

They started off at a brisk pace, Webb aware of the stirring of a new excitement. The more he thought about the herd in Apache Basin and its proximity to the Parker place, the stronger grew his belief that this could be the location where rustlers might strike if a raid on his stock was a real possibility.

He was almost sorry now that he hadn't accepted Mal Jordan's offer and heard what Jordan would have had to say about the rustlers' plans. But he had missed his chance and the man was dead.

64

Apache Basin was in the extreme southwestern tip of Triangle B range. The country was wild and exposed, but provided good summer fodder. In the late fall, the herds were always moved closer to home in preparation for the icy blasts and snowstorms, when feed would have to be carted out in wagons.

Southwards from the basin, the country was bleak and forbidding, backing roughly to a wilderness of cliffs, deep gorges and harsh canyons. It followed that, if rustlers decided to strike at Apache Basin, they would have to drive the cattle north or east. No one in his proper senses would dare challenge the unyielding desert country that characterised the badlands.

Pete Hogan understood all this and cut a trail that would cover a wide section of the basin approaches so that, if a cattle raid was in operation, they were almost bound to intercept the rustlers before they succeeded in making a clear getaway.

A narrow sliver of moon was sailing in the sky when they forded a stream and saw the stark outline of the basin rim before them. Hogan turned his head to catch the hum of the breeze drifting towards them.

'Hear anything?' he queried.

Webb was about to answer in the negative

when a dull, drumming noise caused the air to vibrate, making his mount whistle nervously. He hauled the chestnut in, the better to listen above the wild beating of its heart. The very earth beneath them appeared to shiver. Then there was a chorus of lowing, a sharp, anxious warning, and the next instant a burst of gunfire raged out of the shadows in front of them.

Pete Hogan spurred forward, waving an arm, and Webb sent the chestnut racing in his wake. This was his second trip after rustlers and he hoped that, unlike the last time, he might manage to come to grips with them. Only, what would happen if one of these rogues of the range should turn out to be that pretty girl's rascally brother?

FOUR

Pete Hogan was still in front of Webb when he dropped over the rim of Apache Basin and saw the orange bursts of flame from the guns. The basin was about three miles across, and it seemed as though the rustlers were intent on driving the cattle towards the north. It was minutes before Webb could distinguish the herd: at first he discerned a few head of stock, lumbering frantically this way and that, bawling in misery and fear. Pete Hogan appeared to ride towards the middle of the great natural bowl, the focal point of the commotion. Then Webb saw the main herd, a solid mass of heaving, lunging shadows.

Hogan began triggering into the air, no doubt hoping to fool the thieves into thinking that many more than two Triangle B riders were abroad. Webb joined in, firing until his six-shooter was empty.

He dragged his mount down to re-load, all the while squinting through the gloom, trying to get a clearer view of the operation. A few minutes later he saw one of the rustlers – a shadowy form that dashed away out on his left with the fleetness of an Indian. Webb pulled off to the right flank, with the idea of trying to break the herd's wild run out of the basin.

He had gone only a few hundred yards or so when another horseman swept out of the murk and din. Webb dragged his gun free, raked with indecision, not sure whether the rider was his foreman. But when the man continued to charge down on him and deliberately triggered a shot that blazed past his face, Webb fired, praying that this wasn't Bill Sloan or Dick Cartwright who had been drawn by the noise.

The oncoming rider thundered up and Webb spurred the chestnut savagely, dragging it to one side as the other dashed past. He swivelled to see the horse galloping over a hummock and vanish, and knew for a certainty that the beast had been riderless.

Sweat broke on his brow, but there was no time to work things out. He saw more riders, a compact bunch of cattle. Guns bellowed, and the noise blended with the thudding of hooves and the frightened protests of the cattle. Then he saw two horsemen racing towards him. He heard a screamed curse and had a vision of a man poised in his stirrups, hat in hand, one arm raised. Flame erupted in a blinding flash, and then the chestnut was going into a circle, straightening, and tearing off along the edge of the seething mass of cattle.

Now he heard someone pounding along behind him. He twisted from the waist, Colt lifted to defend himself. A voice tried to make itself heard above the general bedlam.

'Webb!'

'Pete, what in tarnation–'

'Get back, you damn fool or you'll be

ploughed under,' his foreman warned.

Then Pete was swallowed in a smothering rush of dark hides. Webb saw the heaving backs and realized the danger he was in. He had put himself directly in front of the stampeding animals, and if he didn't act quickly he was doomed.

The first of the cattle smashed across the chestnut's flank and the horse whistled in terror. It rose on its hind legs and almost unseated its rider. Webb held on grimly. When the horse came down, stiff-legged on all fours, he drove his heels in. All around him was the sweaty stench of the stampeded herd. Steam rose in clouds. He got the chestnut under way, slithering and skidding on the churned earth. Now he was charging for another group of cattle, but this time they broke in front of the racing horse. Then he was in the open, hearing hoofbeats tearing off into the night.

Indecision clawed at him. His first duty was to try to halt the stampede before the herd had a chance to scatter to all points of the range. He peered around him, hoping to spot Pete Hogan. More guns barked away in his rear. The rustlers kept going, angling for the southern rims of the basin. Their very presence made up his mind for him, and he forked out after them.

He was soon clear of the straggling remnants of the herd and pounding far beyond the cattle, over the rich grazing land. He knew there was a rider up in front of him yonder and out on his right; another appeared intent on making a fast retreat on his left. This one was nearest to Webb and he touched spurs to the chestnut's flanks.

At length the fugitive gained a broken edge of the basin rim that was sharply etched against the lighter backdrop provided by the sky. He appeared to hesitate briefly in the notch, then thrust his mount over. Webb swept up to the rim, where a cold breeze whipped down from the higher reaches. He saw a long slope before him, patched with shadow here and there: tree shadow, rock shadow. Then he glimpsed his quarry and urged the chestnut to the slope.

Ten minutes later Webb realized that he was steadily overtaking the fleeing cattle-thief. The man seemed to be making for a stand of timber rising against the star-shot sky. Once up there, he halted and sent a revolver shot at his pursuer. Webb veered sharply to the left and drew up sharply when he realized that the other must have gone to earth. There was no sign of him now, no sound to pinpoint his position.

Behind Webb, in the basin, the turmoil had diminished to a dull, drumming noise. A horse was tearing off into the north, and the clamour of its hoofbeats soon faded and died. He glimpsed a thicket about a hundred yards ahead of him and sent the chestnut towards it. Gunfire erupted up there on the higher ridges, and bullets raged about him.

He managed to reach the thicket unscathed and dropped from the saddle. The chestnut wanted to break away, but he fought it and secured the reins to a dead snag. Then he drew his Colt and pressed the thorny brush aside to get a better look at the fringe of trees.

At this juncture he had qualms about running away from Pete Hogan. Pete might think he had cleared out altogether when the going became too tough. Webb smiled faintly, reflecting on the foreman's opinion of him.

A stirring in the trees brought him back to the moment.

His eyes narrowed when he picked out a horse shifting into the open. He raised his revolver, judging that the rustler considered it was safe enough to make a break. Webb eased the trigger pressure when he saw that the horse was, in fact, riderless. It trotted off a little, then halted and began to nuzzle at the earth.

Webb's initial reaction was to suspect a trick. The man in there knew he had followed him and believed he was lurking somewhere in the near vicinity. Possibly he hoped to throw Webb off guard to the extent of getting in a telling shot. Despite the loose horse moving further away reins trailing, Webb remained where he was, patient and watchful.

Five minutes dragged by, ten. The muted noise of cattle on the move still drifted from the direction of the basin. The earth where he hunkered was chill with the night dampness, the vegetation sour in his nostrils. He kept watching the line of trees, letting his attention range slowly to the right, then just as slowly to the left. A wind had risen and was making the topmost branches sway. The wind in the trees produced a low, crooning sound that was vaguely disturbing.

Then Webb heard another horse heading eastwards at a gallop, and wondered if that would be Pete or one of the rustlers. The loose horse laid off foraging and came closer. It threw its head up and whickered, chopping the ground with a front hoof.

At the end of another five minutes, Webb

decided to investigate. The thought occurred to him that the rustler might have been wounded and was lying low until he had a chance to drag himself to his mount. Gun at the ready, Webb left the cover of the thicket, surmising that if the man in the shadows intended taking a shot at him, he would do it now. He held himself ready to dive to the earth at the first indication of danger.

Nothing happened, and his brow puckered in puzzlement. The rustler's horse had spotted him and set up a loud whinnying. The chestnut gave an answering whinny and instigated a noisy chorus. The screen of trees up ahead appeared cloaked in impenetrable shadow, and another possibility occurred to Webb. The man in there might have run out of ammunition and was exhibiting greater patience than he, Webb, had shown. He could be lying low with a knife at the ready, waiting for the right chance to strike.

'You're sure letting your imagination get the better of you,' he mused whimsically.

He kept going, picking each step with the utmost care, and when he reached the first massive tree-trunk he halted. Something rustled in the high branches and a night-bird squawked angrily and soared off to roost elsewhere. He began threading a path through the trees. The ground underfoot became soft and somewhat spongy. Pine needles had formed a thick carpet.

When he came on the hunched shape of a man he hauled back a step and pointed his Colt.

'Don't move!'

The man on the ground emitted a low groan, as if he was in great pain. But this could all be part of the deadly subterfuge, and Webb's finger curled on the trigger. Then his toe touched something solid, and when he risked a closer look he saw that it was a revolver. Stooping quickly, he gathered up the weapon and pushed it under his belt.

'All right, mister,' he said brusquely, 'time to rise and shine. I know you're bluffing, and if you keep it up you're going to get a chunk of lead where it'll hurt real bad.'

'Hell, I – can't – move ... I'm shot...'

Something in the tone of that voice struck a responsive chord, and Webb was conscious of a constricting dryness in the walls of his throat. He stooped, revolver poised in his right hand, and with the other hand he investigated, soon feeling a cloying warmth, a dampness that caused the short hairs at the nape of his neck to prickle. Blood.

'Are you really badly hurt?'

'I'm like – to – die,' was the hustled response.

Webb pouched his Colt and produced his matches. He had to strike two before managing to coax a steady flame against the wind soughing among the trees. He cupped the tiny circle of radiance and held it close to the man's face. Even as he did so he was aware of a hard, clawing sensation in the pit of his stomach.

The wounded man was Maureen Parker's brother, Jim.

The flame had scarcely died before Webb heard a horseman pounding up the slope towards them. Pete Hogan, probably searching for his tenderfoot boss, or perhaps one of his crew. If he was discovered here with Jim Parker there would be nothing else for it but to hand the nester's son over to his men. And the way things were at the moment, that could have dire consequences. The cowhands would vote for hanging the rustler or planting a bullet in him. Webb believed he would likely feel like doing that himself in different circumstances. Any rancher knew there was only one effective way to put a cow-thief out of action for good.

But how could he bring himself to hand the girl's brother over to such rough justice?

The horseman was steadily drawing closer, and if he wished to save Parker's hide there was only one course of action open to him. Without further delay he dashed into the open and went after Jim's horse. The beast frustrated his every effort to catch it, leaving him swearing furiously and tempted to bring the brute down with a bullet. The horse whistled shrill defiance and raced away into the darkness. It kept going as if it knew that its master's life might depend on its fleetness and the fact that it must outrun pursuit at all costs.

Webb let it go and looked about for the chestnut. It was out of sight, lurking some-where in the shadows. The approaching rider was almost on top of him now, and he ducked back into the gloom-shrouded trees.

When he came to the spot where he had left Parker, the nester was making a desperate attempt to stand upright.

'Take it easy, damn you,' Webb hissed at him. 'Do you want to die where you are, or be caught?'

Jim Parker lifted a pale, pain-ridden face. 'Who – who...'

'Just keep still,' Webb told him.

He spread a hand for silence as the horse-man tore up to the fringe of trees and began a frantic investigation. His horse was blowing, and he kept sawing on the reins, trying to hold the beast. The harness jingled dully. Webb had a glimpse of white, rolling eyes.

The rider called sharply: 'Boss, are you there?'

Pete Hogan. Webb ground his teeth in an agony of indecision. Then Hogan took his horse off to the right, muttered something, and sent it lunging away at a tangent. But it was merely a temporary respite, Webb felt sure. Pete must have spotted Jim Parker's horse and gone after it. Then he would come back to intensify his search.

There was a lot of stamping and whistling going on. Pete's continued swearing added to the din. The nester stirred and Webb turned to him.

'What is it? I told you to be quiet.'

'You're – Webb – Bannister...'

'I sure as blazes wish I was somebody else right now.'

After a while it appeared that Pete Hogan had no intention of retracing his way, and Webb ventured out of the woods to retrieve his chestnut. He was surprised to see that Jim Parker's mount had somehow made its way back to the wooded ridge, and after five minutes coaxing the beast to stand where it was until he reached it, he was finally able to make a grab for the reins. He brought the horse to where he had left the chestnut tied and took both horses to the trees, peering around him and listening for a signal that would herald the return of Pete.

The night had gone still again, and Webb brought Jim's horse to the clearing where he lay. Parker was surprisingly heavy and Webb was breathing hard by the time he had heaved him high enough to allow him to claw his way into the saddle.

'Whatever happens, hold on,' he warned.

An hour later, Webb was able to see the narrow ribbon of water that was Silver Creek by the pale moonlight. Parker had made no move nor spoken another word, but he was able to hold himself in the saddle, slumped forward, his head lolling from side to side occasionally, so that Webb had to keep the chestnut close by.

Webb had already considered the danger in bringing Jim home like this. His father or sister might get the notion that he had deliberately shot him. And, as far as he could see, Maureen was going to have her work cut out if she was to nurse her brother back to health. Jim could die at any minute, he supposed. He had no way of knowing just how serious the gunshot wound really was.

Approaching the yard, he saw the light still burning in the window. Remembering the way Josh roamed around in the dark, he halted and slapped Jim's mount on the rump. It broke into an excited trot and set up a shrill whinnying.

Webb watched as the front door was opened and someone came out. There was a concerned shout, and he waited no longer. He backed the chestnut to the creek and splashed through the shallows. He heard a shout behind him, but paid no heed. He hugged the line of willows for half a mile or so, then sent the horse into a long lope, heading for Apache Basin once more.

There was a guard on the rim when he arrived, and he was challenged to announce himself. The guard greeted him when he recognized him and told him that Pete Hogan was across the basin somewhere.

'What about Bill Sloan and Dick Cartwright?' Webb queried.

'They're all right, Mr Bannister.' The lookout sounded puzzled. He was probably asking himself where in hell the boss had gotten to, and if he had managed to get over his fright.

Webb could almost read his mind, and he had to curb the raw whip of anger that touched him. 'Were they hurt?'

'Bill got a nick in the arm. Pete sent him and Dick home when he got here.'

'Everything's quiet now?'

'Yeah, we put the bastards on the run.'

There was a little crooked smile at Webb's lips as he continued. Pete must have got a message through to ranch headquarters and had reinforcements sent here. He met another of his men riding guard on the edge of the herd in the basin, and he in turn directed him to the northern slope, where the rustlers had been driving the cattle. He found Pete Hogan eventually with a rider called Slim. He expected some form of blistering reception, but Hogan gave a whoop of welcome.

'Webb!' The use of his name was somehow mollifying to Webb, and he decided to play his cards close to his chest. 'Damn it, we figured you might have been hit,' Pete went on. 'Where did you get to?'

'Took out after one of the bandits. Did they manage to make off with any stuff?'

'Not on your life! Most of it's rounded up again. Quieted down mostly, as you can see.'

'That's great, Pete. You did a good job.' No sooner had Webb mouthed the compliment than he regretted it. The Old Man would have said something like: 'Damn your hide, Pete, I figured you'd have caught some of the so-and-sos...'

So-and-sos? Webb grinned wryly in the darkness. Well, he would just have to go right on learning, he supposed.

'I'm posting three of the boys here for the rest of the night,' Hogan was explaining. 'All right with you?'

'You know best, Mr Hogan.' He was withdrawing to have a look around the edge of the herd when Pete spoke bitingly.

'Cursed nesters have been at it again. Oh, sure, who else do you reckon is doing the stealing? Tweaking our tails. Robbing us blind. Then they have the sass to squat where they've no damn right to set their rumps.'

'Wait a minute,' Webb reasoned. 'You can't blame anybody without proof. You can't accuse anybody without proof.'

'Proof hell, Boss, and you know it fine. Know how many wideloopers were here tonight?'

Webb waited to be told. He had no clear idea how many thieves had descended on the Apache Basin herd.

'Six at least,' Hogan declared emphatically. 'Know what that means?'

Webb felt totally inadequate. He should have some idea, but he would have to work it out for himself. Was Hogan sincere about driving home a valid point, or was he simply showing the Old Man's son to be a hopeless case?

'Means they're banding together,' Pete explained patiently.

'Something will have to be done about it.'

'Something *will* be done,' was the savage response. Then Hogan added in a softer tone, 'You might as well head on home, Boss. I can handle it from here. Boys figure you acted pretty nifty tonight. We'll go into that nester thing in the morning. All right with you?'

'Anything you say, Pete.'

His cheeks were afire as he rode away from Hogan and the rider called Slim, and he was grateful for the darkness that had shielded his face and made it difficult to read his thoughts. Why had Pete not mentioned Jim Parker? Did he suspect what his boss had been up to tonight? The idea brought a bitter oath to Webb's lips. He would have to learn this ranching game, and he would have to learn how to deal with the thieves who were threatening Triangle B stock.

He was in no hurry riding home. There was

too much to think about, too much to work out. And there was the problem of Jim Parker to be taken care of. He arrived back at headquarters eventually and put the chestnut up himself, then headed to the bunkhouse to see Bill Sloan and Dick Cartwright. The cowhands were cheerful enough, and Slim made light of his injury. Both men were preparing to turn in. Three other members of the crew were already in their bunks, sleeping or feigning sleep. Webb decided the latter guess would be closer to the mark, and once again he felt angry and frustrated. He was heading off when Cartwright said slowly: 'These rustlers are getting bolder, Mr Bannister. And we're not the only outfit to suffer.'

'I know, Dick. I'm thinking of riding to Yellow Fork and seeing the sheriff. Only, it's a big range for a lawman to cover.'

'Too big,' the other agreed. He worked the toe of his boot on the floor. 'What I'm really trying to say, Mr Bannister, is that I figure the cowmen will be making their own law before long.'

Webb was about to take him up on this, having no time for the law of the rope. But he didn't think it would be advisable to open an argument just then. He left without commenting and headed for the house.

Tonight, the building seemed larger than ever, more oppressive somehow. It had been so different when the Old Man was here. His father's personality had filled the house, dominated everything. His ghost appeared to haunt the place, hover in the shadows and accuse his son of being weak, of not taking a firm stand behind his foreman and doing what had to be done.

He washed and smoked for a while, thinking he would turn in shortly. He had a feeling that tomorrow might bring even greater strain and a bigger challenge. But when he lay down, it was to twist and turn restlessly. After a while he consulted the clock and saw that it was past three. Morning already! The day started at dawn on a cattle outfit, and in a way he envied the cowboys. They could head off and do their work without having to address problems that at times could appear insurmountable.

Had he been wise taking up where his father had left off? Would he not be happier if he sold the ranch and went back east where he had gone to study law after he and the Old Man failed to see eye to eye on practically everything to do with ranching?

Other thoughts occurred to cancel this proposition out. Ranching was in his blood, of course, and so was this wide, sprawling land. He was exactly where he should be, doing what he was destined to do. In time he would learn the ropes properly and take the actual running of affairs out of Pete Hogan's hands.

He wished Pete would return. Did the foreman intend staying overnight at Apache Basin, in case the rustlers were tempted to come back?

He went out to the veranda and sat on the rocker, a cigar between his lips. He remained there for an hour and, when there was still no sign of Pete Hogan at the end of that time, he crawled under the blankets. He fell asleep almost at once, and dreamed of Maureen Parker.

It was full daylight when Webb awoke, and he lost no time in washing and shaving. Pete Hogan came over to the house after the cook had laid out Webb's breakfast in the dining-room. This morning the foreman looked none too bright, and there was a gauntness about his cheeks that Webb hadn't noticed before. Pete sat down with a faint grin and poured himself a cup of coffee. This had become a morning ritual which Webb found quite pleasant. This morning, however, his stomach felt as if it was coiled up tight, and he was sure he didn't look too spry himself.

'We weren't the only outfit to have rustler trouble last night,' the foreman drawled. 'Just got word that Nate Smith lost somewhere around fifty head of prime stuff.'

Webb whistled softly. 'This is rustling on a big scale then,' he commented.

'Too big. There'll have to be an end to it. The word I got says the ranchers are calling a meeting. They'll let you know the time and place.' Pete's eyes acquired a glint. 'You'll go along?'

Webb's first impulse was to say he wouldn't and make some excuse, but as he watched the old mockery creep in he nodded shortly. 'I guess so.'

'Good. Maybe we can sort something out to clean up this end of the range.' Pete finished his coffee and rose. 'I'm heading for the basin again. Hope to see you around noon. All right?'

Webb nodded again. When the foreman had gone he hunted out a cigar and smoked it, thinking about the ranchers' meeting. He knew what the outcome would be. The way things were shaping, most of the old-timers would demand vigilante justice.

His thoughts shifted to Silver Creek and

Jim Parker. He wondered if Parker's sister and father had been able to do anything for him last night, or if they had to get the doctor from town. By this time Jim might be dead.

He went to the stable and had the hostler saddle the sorrel. The old fellow wanted to jaw about the raid on Apache Basin, but Webb cut his talk short. The herd had been saved, he said, and that was what mattered.

Leaving the ranch buildings, he headed into the south, riding along in a leisurely fashion and trying to fool himself that he had better pay some attention to this end of his graze. When he decided to be honest with himself, however, he pushed the lively sorrel into a run. There was no reason why he shouldn't visit the Silver Creek homestead, and if Jim Parker felt up to it, there were some straight questions he wished to put to him.

The sun was climbing in a flawless blue sky, and the land was fresh and radiant in the new day's light when Webb emerged from the timber and rode down to the shore of the creek. He went through the cottonwoods and willows, and halted abruptly to sniff the air.

He frowned, recognizing the smell. Woodsmoke. Not the trickle to be expected from a fire-pipe, but a solid, throat-catching reek of charred timber. Then realization hit him and he yelled protestingly, sending the sorrel thundering on to the Parker homestead.

He dragged the horse to a grinding stand-still in the yard and stared in horror at the smouldering heap of fire-blackened logs and broken glass. Dismay struck through him with the keenness of a knife blade as he gazed around him.

The Parker house had been burned to the ground.

FIVE

For a long time all Webb could do was sit and stare in shock and revulsion. It appeared that his nerves and muscles had become paralysed. He found it difficult to accept the evidence in front of him. What had happened here? When had the fire started? Who had done this hideous thing?

He pulled himself together and slid from the saddle, then began a frantic search on the fringe of the charred, smoking ruins. The initial shock over, he began to think more calmly. There was no sign of anyone having been caught in the fire. It could just as well have been the result of an accident as a deliberate act of arson. But he knew he was trying to fool himself, trying to make excuses for people who could never be excused.

This was what had kept Pete Hogan out last night. After the Apache Basin raid, Pete had put all the clues together, formed his own conclusions. He might even have suspected that his boss had called here when he should have been fighting for the herd, looking after his own interests and the interests of his employees.

Pete had decided that Jim Parker had been mixed up in the rustling deal; he had brought some of the Triangle B boys down to the creek in order to clear the Parkers right off the land. Where were the Parkers?

The question put a chill in him that swamped out other considerations. What had become of the wounded Jim? What had become of old Josh? Where was Maureen at this very minute?

What would she think of him now?

He began to search. The earth about the homestead was tamped so hard it was difficult to pick up tracks, much less read them. When he had worked his way round to the place where the chicken run was located, he saw the fence down. There was no livestock in sight. Nothing. The Silver Creek homestead was deserted.

If this really turned out to be Pete Hogan's work he would fire him. His foreman had appeared tired and drawn earlier, but he had given Webb no hint of what had happened to the nester family. Likely Pete calculated that his boss would head this way this morning and find out for himself what had taken place.

'I'll murder him,' Webb whispered hoarsely.

He searched around until he came on the tracks of wagon wheels close to the shore of the creek, and saw that the Parkers must have travelled southwards. He climbed into the saddle and put the sorrel into motion, taking a last look at the burnt-out hulk that still seethed and crackled and gave off sparks and little puffs of black smoke.

He rode for an hour into the southern tip of Triangle B graze, came on the creek off-shoot that provided a boundary marker between his land and that owned by Will Johnson who had his Lazy J headquarters about ten miles to the west of the water-course. It was apparent that the Parkers had followed the off-shoot, wishing to remain close to water. He wondered how far they would carry the wounded Jim, wondered whether Jim was alive or dead.

The creek meandered out of the plains and twisted towards a stretch of woodland. The wagon tracks continued along the bank. Webb surveyed the land behind him. The sun was well up by this time and a brittle heat hung heavy on the still air. He began to have doubts about the wisdom of trailing the Parkers. What good could come of it? What could he do to help the family when he found them?

He slowed when he reached the timber, catching the pungent odour of wood-smoke, this scent an innocent and wholesome thing. Then he glimpsed the wagon in a glade and a small tent contrived from a sheet of canvas. Wood-smoke curled aloft, and he caught his breath when he spotted the girl stooped over a fire, a frying pan in her hand.

He was on the point of withdrawing to a safer distance when Josh Parker called to him from the cover of a tree-trunk. 'I see you, Bannister! Come on in here.'

There was no mistaking the hostile determination in the tone. Webb saw the barrel of the rifle that was aimed at him and nudged the sorrel into the glade, hands in plain sight. The girl placed the pan aside and straightened as he rode up. Parker shifted from his hiding place. He looked ragged, somewhat furtive, but there was a look about him that boded ill for an enemy.

'Hello again, Josh.'

'Hello again nothing!' the other snarled. 'I'm going to give you a half minute to say your prayers before I drill you.'

If they expected Webb to plead for his life they were mistaken. His eyes moved from the girl to her father, and when he spoke his voice was edged with angry impatience.

'Put that damned gun away, Parker, or I'll be tempted to wrap it around your ears.'

They gaped at him in silence. Parker's lips moved, but speech refused to emerge, and while he was dithering, Webb dismounted and draped the reins carefully over the sorrel's face. He fingered out his tobacco and began to build a cigarette. The girl went on staring at him. She was pale, worn looking. Certainly the strain of last night had left its mark.

'What about Jim?' he asked her.

'He's alive,' she replied coldly. 'No thanks to your men.'

'Who – who fired your house?'

Parker swore luridly at this and the rifle swung up once more. 'As if you didn't know! Damn it, Reen, I can't take much more from this critter.'

'Hold on, Dad,' she said quickly. There was puzzlement in her eyes at this juncture. 'Wasn't it you who brought Jim home last night after – after...'

Webb nodded. 'I did. My men and I were fighting with a gang that tried to steal our herd in Apache Basin. I'm sorry to tell you that your brother was one of the raiders.'

Her head fell forward and she held her hand to her mouth. Then she looked directly at the visitor while a little colour crept into her cheeks. 'Mr Bannister, you – you must forgive Jim if you can find it in you to do so. He got into bad company, and–'

'Quit talking,' her father snarled at her. 'You don't have to crawl to anybody. Your brother's old enough to stand on his own feet and take his own medicine. He'll get over the gun hurt.'

'He mightn't get over a rope as easily,' Webb reminded him drily.

'You've no room to talk,' the homesteader flung at him. 'Anyhow, who's saying you're going to leave here alive?'

Webb glared at him. 'You're no gunman, Parker, so don't try fooling yourself that you are. Now, if you don't mind, I'd like to hear what happened at your place last night.'

'He's bluffing,' Parker ranted before his daughter could say anything. 'Bannister, I don't care to have you hanging round my girl. Not after what–'

'Dad!'

'Oh, hell, I'm sick of all this talking,' her father complained wearily. 'Bannister, are we still on your land?'

'You're on Lazy J,' Webb told him. 'And from what I know and hear of Will Johnson, that could be a lot worse.'

'Don't you believe it, sonny. Anybody who'd order an old man and his daughter to shift in the middle of the night ain't worth shucks in any language.'

Webb addressed the girl. 'Was it my foreman?'

'The one called Hogan and two others,' she replied evenly. 'They wanted to know how Jim got shot, and I told them Dad had done it accidentally when they were out hunting. I know that your foreman didn't believe me. One of the others wanted to take Jim to Yellow Fork, but he would have died on the way.'

'How is he?'

'It's just a bad flesh wound.' She indicated the tent with her head. 'He should recover all right.'

'Tell me what happened when Pete got to your place.'

'We were ordered to pack the wagon with anything we could carry. They helped us. Moving Jim was the worst part of it. We hadn't gone far when we smelt the smoke and saw the flames. They – they must have burned the house...' She broke off and sobbed. She had gone to a lot of trouble to make the Silver Creek place habitable. She had believed she was making something that might endure. Now she and her father and brother were back where they had started.

The chickens clucked in crates. The gaunt cows were foraging through the trees. Parker had evidently postponed his decision to kill the visitor and placed his rifle against a tree while he tamped tobacco into his pipe. There was a low call from the tent and the girl hurried to it and ducked inside.

Webb scratched the back of his neck, glanced at Parker and found that worthy regarding him morosely. He got his pipe going, puffed fiercely.

'I just can't figure you out, Bannister. Why are you bothering with us like this? Your own men are against us, and the way I see it, your foreman totes your whip.'

The taunt made Webb wince. But perhaps he should have expected something of the sort. He countered: 'If you were in my boots, what would you do?'

That threw the homesteader off balance for a moment. He fidgeted nervously, spat amber juice at a stone. 'Hell, I don't know. Maybe you're right to drive us off your land. And another thing I want you to know: I don't go along with Jim keeping company with that bunch of rascals.'

'Unless Jim mends his ways he's going to end up with his neck in a noose,' Webb warned heavily. 'Don't forget, you're on Johnson's territory, like I told you. His men have the reputation for stamping out rustlers like flies. Why don't you make for Yellow Fork, where there's proper law? It's not fair on your girl to keep her tramping all over the country.'

'Ha, so that's the way the wind blows! If it wasn't for Reen you wouldn't give a damn about Jim and me. Am I right?'

Webb didn't hesitate long over his reply. 'I reckon you are, Mr Parker.'

'So you're soft on my girl, huh?'

The girl's appearance from the tent gave Webb the excuse for refusing to answer. Her eyes were clouded with worry.

'How is he?' Webb asked her.

'Not too good.'

'Mind if I have a look at him?'

'I don't think ... I–' She looked at her father, but Parker was not disposed to object or argue.

Webb tugged his hat off and entered the tent. It was shadowy, and there was the smell of iodine, and he soon made out the form of Jim Parker on a makeshift cot, covered with a blanket. Jim summoned a sour smile.

'I heard you were here. Have you come to finish me off?'

'May I have a look at the wound?'

'Damned if you can, Bannister. I don't want any handouts from your ilk. I can look after myself.'

'Sure you can. With pink ribbons.' Webb hunkered beside him, his features grim. 'You cock an ear to what I have to say, Jim. You're riding for a big fall. It wouldn't matter a curse if you were on your own, but you've got a sister and a father to consider.'

That elicited a harsh laugh. Parker coughed, grimaced, but the hard smile came back to his lips.

'What's it to you anyhow? You're just gloating over us like a fat buzzard. Sure you are! The big cowman riding around like some of them knights out of the story books! Pretending to be big-hearted, to be interested in us nesters. And all the time you stand back and let your man do the dirty work you're too lily-livered to do yourself.'

Webb's jaw hardened. Parker's words hit him like bullets, and he was forced to consider how much truth might be in them.

'You'd better give your rustling pards the slip, mister. If you don't, you're going to end up dead. I think I nailed one of the thieves in the basin last night. But I can't be sure. I'm not even sure that it wasn't one of my slugs that hit you.'

Parker tried to laugh, but it hurt too much. 'Don't flatter yourself, Bannister. You can't shoot that straight. I was hit before you came after me, else I could have got rid of you easy enough.' His words tailed away. Twin spots of unhealthy colour stained his cheeks. Then he added: 'I'm not finished with you, mister, and don't fool yourself that I am. Another thing ... stay away from my sister. If you don't, I'll kill you. I aim to kill you anyhow.'

Webb lifted his head suddenly, hearing hoofbeats. Someone appeared to be riding towards the homesteaders' camp site. Jim Parker's eyes glittered.

'So you brought your men after all? Well,

what can you expect from a damn coyote?'

Webb ignored him and flipped the canvas flap open. He ducked outside to see three rough-looking riders hauling up close to the wagon. His heart plunged, and his hand was falling to his holstered gun when something warned him to be careful. He recognized the tall man whom he had seen with Jim Parker, the one called Singleton. The other two were strangers. No sooner did it register with Singleton who he was than he swept his six-shooter up.

'Hey, this is a Triangle B man!'

'No!' a squat range tramp cried in mock surprise. He showed yellowed teeth in an evil sneer. 'But what's he doing here?'

'We'll soon find out. Hoist them, Mr Bannister.'

Webb raised his arms slowly, regarding each of the rangehawks in turn. Maureen was standing over to the left of the fire while her father took up a position opposite her. A low cry sounded from the tent.

'Single, is that you?'

'Sure enough, Jim pard!' McCall returned. He dismounted and side-stepped Webb to reach the canvas structure. Passing the girl, he touched her chin with his forefinger, causing her to back away quickly. McCall chuckled and gestured to his friends. 'Keep this Bannister jasper covered.'

He emerged from the tent shortly, a sly grin warping his tight mouth. He moved over to where Webb stood, circled him slowly. He halted in front of him and scratched his jaw with his gun barrel.

'You gave us quite a runaround last night, Mr Bannister. Too bad we lost the beeves.'

This appeared to be a signal for the other two to slide from their horses and move across. Webb swallowed thickly, not liking the manoeuvre. He was tempted to draw his gun and try to down one or two of them before they got him. His fate was plain in Singleton McCall's eyes.

'McCall, I'm going to give you a piece of good advice,' he told the outlaw in a slow, measured tone. 'You and your men get on your horses and clear out of here.'

The rustler threw his head back and laughed. 'Happens we're on Lazy J land, Mr Bannister, and that ain't no concern of yours at all. In fact, if anybody's trespassing here it's you.' The forced humour receded from his face and his voice hardened. 'We rode past Silver Creek on our way here. Your boys made a good job of the burning.'

'I didn't order it.'

'The hell you didn't! So you crawl when you're caught flat-footed on your own? Makes a big difference being on your own, don't it? You'd maybe get the notion I'm scared of a big gent like you. But I ain't a damn bit. Want to know something, Mr High and Mighty, I'm ready to take you up on the challenge you threw out when you beat Jim... Get that belt off quick!'

Webb hesitated, touching dry lips with his tongue. McCall's coyotes were on either side, revolvers drawn, expecting a feast of excitement.

'Better get it off, Mr Bannister,' McCall grated. 'Real quick, sonny.'

Webb complied, and let his gun and belt fall to the ground. He sought Maureen's eyes for a brief instant and saw how they burned with a queer fascination. Parker was puffing at his pipe, trying to appear unruffled.

No sooner had Webb's revolver struck the earth than McCall smashed his left fist into his mouth.

Webb stumbled backwards. He was trying to gather himself when the other two came at him. He lashed out and caught the squat one flush on the jaw. He was slamming a hard, looping blow at the man on his right when McCall hit him again in the stomach.

Then the three of them were closing on him, clawing, striking, pounding. A gun barrel smote his head and dropped him to the ground. A boot crunched into his chest, and once more Webb was flung backwards.

He made a desperate attempt to recover, to prevent his senses from slipping away from him. He sucked hungrily for air and saw the three faces as a single leering mask.

He knew when something small and hard and cold was laid against his left temple. The clicking of a hammer being cocked was like a knell of doom.

'So long, Bannister...'

'Hold it!'

The gun remained held to his temple, and he knew that the slightest move would have that muzzle spouting. The interference made McCall glance over his shoulder at Josh Parker.

'What's eating you, Pop?'

'Get away from him,' Parker said flatly. 'Go on, unless you want your head cleaned off like a turkey's.'

'You've got to be funning, old man. Jim said to–'

'Never mind what Jim said. The hell with Jim. The hell with you too, McCall, and your cowardly ways. Back off, I tell you, or you're buzzard bait.'

The revolver was slowly withdrawn from Webb's head. Singleton McCall straightened and Webb endeavoured to bring what was going on into focus. Dimly, he saw Josh Parker with his rifle levelled at the three newcomers. One of them had raised his arms.

'You gonna drop your gun, McCall?' Parker snarled.

'I'm taking you for a crazy old coot,' the rustler fumed.

The rifle exploded and McCall leaped, and for an instant Webb was certain that Parker had killed the man. Then the revolver fell from the lean man's fingers and he threw his arms aloft.

'That's better,' Josh Parker applauded with ragged humour. 'Don't take all that much to flush the guts out of coyotes like you. Now get your horses and clear off. Don't come back.'

'But, mister–'

'Damn it, do you think I'm fooling?' Parker screeched. 'Do it.'

Webb let his body sag down. He heard the rattle of saddle gear and the stamping of hooves. Jim Parker shouted weakly from the tent where he lay.

'What's going on?'

Webb heard the three horses leaving the glade at a brisk trot. He pushed himself into a sitting position, then heaved on upright until he was on his feet. He swayed and almost fell, steadied, and moved towards his sorrel. He gripped the bridle reins and hung on to them, head resting against the horse.

'Mr Bannister, are – are you all right?'

He essayed a weak grin, nodded. 'Tell your dad thanks, Maureen. He's a brave old prairie wolf.'

It required three attempts before his toes were in the bow of the stirrup, then he dragged himself into leather, settled, and twined the reins around his right hand. He heard the girl and her father talking urgently, heard Jim calling from the tent. All Webb wanted just then was to get away from them until he had licked his sores and regained some semblance of control.

He touched the sorrel with his heels and it went into a trot. Every heave and pitch sent agony flowing through his body and he gritted his teeth, telling himself that he mustn't let go, must not surrender to the weakness.

He had a feeling presently of being in the open, then the horse was wading through water, and he relaxed somewhat. The sorrel would take him home if he let it have its head. He would make it unless he ran into Singleton McCall and his cronies again, and unless his head exploded under the pressure that wanted to burst through his skull.

A long time later he heard hoofbeats coming towards him. Instinct took over and he fumbled for his revolver. When the riders were almost on top of him he raised his head from the sorrel's neck to see two men loping in on his left flank. He raised his Colt and prepared to fire. Wait until they're almost here, he told himself, then let them have it when you can't miss.

'Webb!' a high voice called. 'Hey, watch what you're doing...'

It got through to him just before his finger squeezed the trigger that this was not an enemy, but his own foreman, Pete Hogan, and therefore there was nothing to fear, no reason to shoot.

He let the hand holding the gun drop, tried to get the weapon back into its sheath. But it slipped past the opening in the leather and fell to the earth. Webb wasn't even aware of this, nor did he know when Pete Hogan dismounted – just in time – to grab him before he hit the ground.

SIX

A cowhand turned up at Triangle B next morning with a message from Nate Smith. A meeting of the cowmen was scheduled for eight o'clock that night in the back room of the Buffalo Head, in Yellow Fork. Could the messenger take it for granted that Webb Bannister, or a representative with the authority to make decisions on behalf of the Triangle B, would be there?

Paul Hogan was present when Webb talked with the messenger, and Hogan nodded firmly. 'Sure, the boss will be there. It's high time the ranchers got together to do something about the rustling. Ain't you for the meeting, Boss?'

Webb agreed to go. It was expected of him and it would look very strange if he failed to turn up and speak his mind on the problem. Since yesterday, his feelings towards the homesteaders and the shady riders drifting about the range had undergone a drastic change. These men might throw up their shanties on the grassland and call themselves

106

settlers or farmers, but in the main he now saw all this as a ruse to blanket their real activities – preying on the ranchers' beef herds.

Pete had begged him yesterday to confess the identity of the men who had beaten him up. He had told the foreman of running into three strange horsemen and of them getting the drop on him. He gave no hint about where the fracas had taken place, and Hogan had expressed his disgust in an outburst of colourful expletives. Pete had admitted to clearing the Parkers off the creek location and setting fire to the homestead.

'It wasn't their place anyhow,' he declared defensively. 'The buildings were there when they squatted.'

Webb didn't have the heart to take him to task at this juncture. He needed time to think the whole business over, reappraise things.

He was stiff and sore that morning, but he rode out with the foreman to make one of his periodic assessments of the work that was going on. They nooned at a line-camp far to the east of headquarters, and then described a rough circle that took them north and west and, finally, dipping south in the slanting afternoon sunshine.

Things were going pretty well for Triangle B in spite of the rustling forays, and Webb felt a certain pride in ownership. As they dipped towards Silver Creek his thoughts shifted to the Parkers and the three hard-cases who had roughed him up yesterday. Had he given Singleton McCall's name to Pete there was no doubt that the foreman would have organized a search right away. That might be a good move in itself, as McCall and his cronies were the type of range buzzards that had to be eliminated sooner or later. The link between McCall and the Parkers was, however, something Webb was reluctant to disclose. Pete might believe the Parkers had gone on out of the country and would make no more trouble.

When they drew close to the boundary dividing Johnson's land from Triangle B they met a couple of Lazy J cowboys. They greeted Webb in a friendly fashion and chatted about grass and water. It was a good year so far and everybody would benefit.

'If we get rid of these damn rustlers,' Pete Hogan qualified grimly. 'Is Will going to the meeting tonight?'

'Reckon so, Pete. Say, want to hear something?' the speaker added with a grin. 'We gave a nester family a quick send-off this morning. Wouldn't you say it was some do, Tom?' he chuckled to his companion.

'Sure thing, Hex, but I couldn't help feeling sorry for that gal.'

'Gal!' the one called Hex erupted in sardonic amusement. 'That was a female cougar, pard. Say, Pete, she ripped right into us, beat the boss all over the face.'

A band of steel seemed to coil in Webb's stomach as he listened. He was about to put a question when he became aware of Hogan's eyes probing him like knife blades. He coloured and tried not to listen to the rest of the cowboys' chatter. They said so long presently and angled away across their own graze.

A few minutes later Hogan said in a neutral voice:

'That was the Parkers they were talking about. They must have shifted on to Johnson's grass. What a laugh!'

Webb refused to be baited. He wished Pete would let the subject drop, once and for all. But Hogan hadn't finished.

'That Jim Parker was in the stolen beef business to his ears,' he commented. 'It's plain as day. Pity about the girl, though.'

Webb kept his eyes averted. They went as far as the Silver Creek location, lingered there for a while, and then switched out for home. Arriving, Webb washed and donned a clean shirt. He ate in the kitchen with Pete and two of the day men who had just come in. Afterwards, he had Jed saddle up a grulla, and was turning across the yard when Hogan appeared.

'Mind if I ride to town with you?'

It was on the tip of Webb's tongue to object, but he curbed his irritation. He would simply have to learn to cope with his foreman's wile and his proclivity for trying to read his mind.

'Of course not. Maybe you'd better hear what they have to say.'

They left headquarters in the warm evening glow, striking the stage road three miles to the east and facing towards Yellow Fork. Most of the journey was made in silence. Hogan appeared preoccupied and rode a little distance in front of Webb. For Webb's part, he was trying to imagine what kind of meeting this would turn out to be. He hoped that the word 'vigilante' would not crop up. Even considering the possibility brought a sour taste to his mouth. In Yellow Fork, they turned their mounts into the livery, and Pete said he would like to pay a visit to a saddle shop, if it was still open. They had about thirty minutes to kill until eight o'clock, and Webb was glad of what he saw as an interlude.

He strolled along the main street in the dregs of the dying day's heat, viewing store windows. He found himself presently at the front of a millinery establishment where the latest ladies' fashions were on display. Moving on past, he was aware of a slow heat lifting through his temples. For a brief moment he had pictured Maureen Parker in one of the creations, with suitable clothing to match. It was a crazy idea, of course, and he tried to brush it out of his mind. Nevertheless, a vision of the girl persisted until he decided that a drink of beer might bring about a clearer and more sensible perspective.

The saloon he chose was the Red Steer, and when he entered it it was fairly well filled with customers, mostly cowhands, noisy, and discussing the meeting ahead of them. He moved in at the end of the counter and ordered a beer. He was drinking it when he overheard someone mentioning his name in a low voice. He frowned, seeing that several heads were being turned in his direction.

Someone chuckled and he heard a snatch of what one of the cowmen was saying. '...only wasting his time. That's right ... a dude rancher that figures hoemen are long-lost cousins...'

The speaker's companion laughed. But it was a nasty laugh, edged with real malice. Then: 'You can't deny she's a sweet enough dame, pard. But I bet she's plain dynamite underneath her...' The rest was lost in a burst of ribald amusement.

Webb's cheeks burned. He placed his glass on the bar and stepped to the man who had spoken last. He was lanky, leathery-skinned puncher, and Webb touched his arm.

'Excuse me...'

'Why, if it ain't Mr Bannister! Well, howdy, Bannister. In for the meeting? Reckon you might know some of us critters. Lazy J–'

Something in Webb's eye caused him to break off. He had been holding out his right hand, and he appeared baffled when the Triangle B owner ignored it.

'What's your name?' Webb asked him curtly.

'My name? Shucks, Mr Bannister, I figured you'd have heard of Skeeter Flynn. Ain't you going to shake hands with a neighbour? Maybe you think I've got scarlet fever or something?'

'Howdy, Flynn.'

'That's all?' the cowhand demanded when Webb merely continued his gelid, remorseless scrutiny. 'Say, maybe you didn't like what I was saying about the Parker filly...'

'Shut your dirty mouth,' Webb hissed.

'Now see here, Mr Bannister, sir, that ain't no way to talk to us gents.'

'I'm talking to you, Flynn. If your friends are as mealy-mouthed and foul-tongued as you, then it applies to them also.'

'So that's it! Folks was just saying you were a damn nester-lover.'

Webb's bunched right fist exploded in Skeeter Flynn's face. The hard, meaty impact blinded Flynn, sent him teetering away from the counter. Card-players at a nearby table hastily grabbed their money and backed off.

Flynn gathered himself and crouched, blood trickling from his nose and mouth. He had the expression of an enraged bull – nostrils wide, small, bloodshot eyes glittering with malevolent intent.

'I'm gonna tear you apart, Mr Bannister...'

Webb said nothing, just moved slightly as Flynn rushed, missed his target, and finished up slamming against the edge of the counter. There, he doubled over, cursing thickly, trying to recover his breath. Webb's left fist came in and clubbed him on the side of his neck, sending him tumbling gracelessly among his friends.

They hooted their appreciation, and one of them gripped Flynn and flung him at the cool and patient tormentor.

This time Flynn thrust a short, wicked blow to the pit of Webb's stomach. He followed through quickly, sweeping his knee into the rancher's groin. Webb had been backing off, with the result that some of the momentum was burned out by the time the knee connected. He was rocked up on his heels, nevertheless, and Flynn lost no time in making the most of his advantage.

He hammered at Webb's body and face, and the Triangle B owner retreated until his shoulders were leaning on one of the stout roof supports. Flynn's next punch was on its way when Webb ducked neatly and the cowhand's knuckles crumpled on the, heavy timber. Flynn roared in pain. He swung around and was hammered on the base of the neck. Then, as he lost balance and started to fall, Webb launched his own knee into the man's ribs, then smashed his boot into his chest. Flynn hit the floor on his face, grovelled and groaned and mumbled oaths. Finally, he surrendered all interest in the proceedings and rolled over in a heap.

Webb brushed lank hair from his forehead

and eyes and turned to the counter. Three of Skeeter Flynn's friends had hung on there while the rest of the customers had chosen to watch from the walls of the bar-room.

One of Flynn's colleagues took a step forward.

'Like to do that all over again, Mr Bannister?'

'Oh, no!' Webb gulped for breath, realizing that he would never be a match for these range devils when it came to vindictiveness and cunning. His chest heaved painfully; his knuckles sang as if they had been in contact with a hot branding iron. His aching shoulder and arm muscles needed a rest.

The speaker was short and chunkily-built, and no doubt saw himself as the last remaining bastion of the Lazy J's honour and glory. He was constructed like a young buffalo, with enough shaggy hair to justify the comparison.

He threw a blow at Webb before he had time to gather his wits, much less think of an answer. His fist caught Webb in the chest with such force and accuracy that it threw him over one of the card-tables, the wood shivering and cracking and collapsing, to deposit the cattleman amid the wreckage. The buffalo's tactics were even more terrible than Flynn's. Without giving Webb a second to collect himself, he sent his spurred boot driving against his ribs. Webb was obliged to yell to scatter the spasm of agony that lanced through him. He rolled wildly as the boot flashed in once more, rolled and reached out, and caught the cowhand's ankle, then twisted with the sort of savagery he had never known was lodged in him.

He dragged the buffalo into the sawdust while a welcome flow of energy streaked through his muscles and nerves. He wrapped his left arm around the man's thick neck, closed the vice, and bludgeoned him on the face with his balled fist until he thought the head must surely fall off. He released the cowhand as quickly as he had trapped him, sprang upright, and was beautifully poised when the man lumbered up to look around him and bring the scene back into focus.

During the next few minutes the occupants of the Red Steer seemed to hold their breaths. The silence was broken only by Webb Bannister's stentorian breathing, the cowhand's efforts to gulp air into his own tortured lungs, and the steady rhythmic slugging of balled fists finding a soft stomach, an unprotected jawline, a bloodied, bulging eye, and slack lips that looked as though they might never come together properly again.

Finally it was over. The buffalo lay like one of his kind when the heavy slug from a Sharps rifle had laid it low. Webb had no more interest in him. He put his back to the two creatures he had thrashed and signalled to the white-faced bartender. When he had a foaming schooner gripped between both hands he declared loudly, and with perhaps a touch of forgivable bravado: 'Plenty more room on the floor, boys. Come on and get it.'

The challenge hung in the air like something charged with the force of lightning. There was a weak, tremulous laugh from someone overcome by the excitement. Someone else raised a weak cheer, and yet someone else clapped with genuine appreciation and respect.

Webb mustered a crooked smile for everybody before it faded and he looked grey and grim and disenchanted with the whole proceedings. He scooped up his hat and pulled it on. His revolver had worked loose, and he regarded it ruefully before pushing it into his holster. He realized there was a lot of blood on his hands, his knuckles. He was scarcely aware of the doors being thrust aside and someone coming in. Then he saw

Pete Hogan. The foreman looked as he had never seen him before. His eyes seemed to stare right through his boss. There was an expression on his face that might have been reserved for times when he came in front of a picture of Abraham Lincoln. Then that, too, vanished, and Webb knew that, from that moment on, Pete and he might always be complete strangers to each other.

Next, he and Hogan were out in the street, and when he would have staggered, the foreman stretched a hand which Webb quickly brushed aside.

'Well, what in hell was all that about?' the older man demanded in the tone he would use to rebuke a child. 'You know what might have happened if you'd killed those two *hombres?*'

'You'd get a real kick out of seeing a rope around my neck, Pete.'

'Hell, I just can't make you out at all. Know what struck me when I saw you standing there, spitting fire and brimstone?'

Webb pretended disinterest, but he was curious to hear all the same. 'Haven't got an idea what struck you.'

'The Old Man,' Hogan declared. 'Just like his ghost had come back to haunt me.'

'Better watch out then,' Webb said drily.

'Look ... I'll have to clean up before that meeting.'

'Good idea. Not much time left. But I'd better warn you that when Johnson hears what you did to his boys...'

Webb made a gesture indicating that he wished to drop the subject. The sun was travelling towards the west. More riders were drifting into Yellow Fork. Webb wondered if they were all here on account of the meeting in the Buffalo Head. A dozen or so horses were already racked in front of the building. Noise streamed over the batwing doors like a torrent that would be hard to abate. Then Webb noticed something else that made him frown.

'Pete, are those all cowmen?'

Hogan squinted across the road to where a group of perhaps a score of men lounged in the shadows at the front of the Whiskey Keg. He gave an angry snort.

'Well, I'll be damned! Nesters. They're getting bold as brass. And yonder's Buff Kane letting on to keep an eye on every-body. I bet he's wishing right now the cow-men had picked some other town for their meeting.'

Webb spotted the tall, stockily-built law-man leaning against the wall of a drug store.

119

Pete touched his sleeve as one of the home-steaders detached himself from the rest of his group and angled towards them.

'Here's Tap Grant,' Hogan said tautly. 'Watch your step.'

Grant was long, spindly. He was dressed in work-worn denims and wore a stained, flat-brimmed hat slanted across his right eye. He drew up in front of the triangle B men and his clear grey eyes fastened on Webb.

'Excuse me, Mr Bannister, could I have a word with you?'

Webb felt slightly flustered. 'Sure. What's the problem?'

'I take you're in town for the meeting in the Buffalo Head saloon, Mr Bannister?'

Webb was becoming acutely aware of the many glances being cast in his direction. Sheriff Kane gave his belt a hitch up around his thick middle and strolled closer. He was curious the way a fox was curious, and likely he suspected there might be trouble which should be nipped in the bud. On his approach, Pete Hogan coughed in an exaggerated manner and spat, making a blatant display of his distaste for the farmer with Webb.

'All right,' Hogan nudged Tap Grant. 'Clear your chest, 'cause we're in a hurry.'

A tide of dark colour swept through the farmer's rugged features, but his eyes remained steadfastly on Hogan's boss. 'I just want to say to you, Mr Bannister, that this rustling can't all be laid at the feet of the homesteaders. You're kind of new, and I feel it's my duty to tell you that. Most of us are family men. We're honest, and just want to make a living for ourselves and our children.'

'I'm not a judge, Grant,' Webb replied somewhat stiffly. He was weary, and he ached all over. He wished he could be left alone in a hot tub for an hour. 'But I've lost cattle myself, and I certainly don't like it. Tell me when you're here, do you know a man called Singleton McCall?'

'A coyote.' Grant shot a quick look at Buff Kane, who was keeping to the sidelines. 'I've heard that he runs a gang and likes to blame the settlers for his mischief-making.'

It was on Webb's lips to tell him about Jim Parker and then ask him if he would like to revise his opinion of the nesters. But he bit the words back. He was feeling more uneasy by the minute. Yet there was one thing he had to get straight, and this was as good a time as any.

'Look, Grant,' he began. 'I believe I'm supposed to have earned the name of being a nester-lover, whatever that means. I'm no so-called nester-lover, but I don't think I could be called a nester-hater either.'

'I take you for a fair man, Bannister. I'm asking you to bring your fair-mindedness to the meeting. It's all I *do* ask of you.'

There was a quality about the lean man that impressed Webb. He recalled the beating he had taken yesterday, recalled the fracas in the Red Steer. Hogan broke in.

'The boss is only one man, Grant, and he has the interests of his ranch at heart.'

'I'm just appealing to his good sense, Hogan.'

'Drift,' Pete said laconically, tucking his thumbs into his shell-belt. He gave Webb a nudge with his elbow and walked on. Webb went after him, knowing that Tap Grant's eyes were on his back. He felt acutely uncomfortable, angry with Pete for his display of discourtesy and bad manners.

'He struck me as a pretty decent sort,' he muttered to the foreman when he caught up.

'Decent all right,' the other growled. 'When they feel the heat growing under them. Don't let them soften you up, Boss. He wouldn't pick on Nate Smith like that, or Johnson.'

They went to a hotel where Webb cleaned

up while Hogan scanned the clerk's reading material in the lobby. In the street again, Sheriff Kane pulled a couple of squabbling men apart, a nester and a cowboy. The lawman lectured them both. The cowhand withdrew to his pards, unforgiving and still belligerent; the farmer walked slowly to his waiting friends.

One of the cowmen shouted drunkenly: 'Let's clear them the hell out of town, boys!'

Webb caught his breath as Buff Kane walked directly to the speaker and grabbed his arm. Kane was soon surrounded by a group of cowmen, all talking angrily at once. Webb blinked when Kane broke out of the gathering with his prisoner and led him down the street to the jailhouse. The cowmen started jeering, and the situation had all the potential of gun-powder. A small spark would cause the whole thing to erupt into a shooting battle.

The farmers retreated a short distance along the road, came together again, no doubt holding a hurried conference.

'This meeting's a bad thing, Pete,' Webb said heavily. 'The nesters know what might come out of it. Vigilante law. Buff Kane has plenty of nerve, and he might be a big man in his own town, but this friction could spread all over the range.'

'Sooner the better,' Hogan grunted. 'But it's the first time I've seen the hoemen banding together. It shows what they might try. Say, it's time we were getting along to the Buffalo Head...'

When they reached the big saloon they made their way through the packed bar-room to a door at the end of the counter. It stood open, and Webb entered with Pete on his heels. This room was comparatively small, with a table in the middle of the floor and a dozen chairs of different shapes and styles ranged around it. Webb counted eight men sitting talking. There were two bottles of whiskey in evidence, and most of the cattle-men were drinking, or had glasses in front of them.

Hogan and his boss received perfunctory greetings and were asked to sit down. They picked chairs near the doorway, and Webb started in to fashion a cigarette. He was soon contributing to the heavy pall of grey smoke that swirled around the ceiling lamps. Two more ranchers came in presently and then the door was closed and the meeting called to order.

Will Johnson acted as chairman and stated tersely the reason for their being together like this. He looked over at Webb and smiled coldly as he added: 'And I'm sure we all welcome John Bannister's son among us.

'Now, gentlemen, I guess you've all seen the show of strength put up by the nesters in town. I want you to view their presence here in its proper light. They're serving warning on us, gentlemen, of what we might expect if we make any resolutions here tonight that means they have to clear off the grass. What they're doing, in effect, is daring us to act in our own interests...'

Johnson could hardly be called an inspired orator. He droned on and on until Webb thought he would never stop. Nate Smith was the next speaker, but Smith gave forth at shorter length and sat down with a flat injunction hanging like lead in the air.

'Let's make our own law on this range!'

Two other ranchers had their say. They talked mostly about the number of cattle they had lost and the steps they had taken to foil the rustlers.

'But it means we have to keep men doing nothing but patrolling the grass,' Ben Ferris declared angrily. 'And that ain't the best way to keep an outfit standing on its hind legs.'

Will Johnson decided to come in after them. Johnson had drunk three glasses of whiskey since Webb's arrival, and he kept darting sharp glances at the Triangle B men. Webb deduced that he knew about the fight in the Red Steer.

'It's no use telling ourselves we don't know who the wideloopers are,' he said thickly. 'We know who they are and we're turning a blind eye on them. I tell you, men, it's these dirt farmers, and it's no use being soft with them...'

It went on and on. Pete Hogan poured a measure of whiskey into the glass at his elbow and drank a little. Webb hadn't touched the stuff, but as time went on he was tempted to indulge, if only to combat the monotony. He had the sensation of being among a pack of wolves that were whipping themselves into a frenzy. It wasn't a healthy thing to behold or take part in, but then the whole atmosphere here had a touch of the bizarre. He wished he had by-passed the meeting in the first place, or let Pete come in his stead. The outcome was already decided although, as yet, no one had made a specific proposal.

A stout man whom Webb knew as Breck Hollis lumbered to his feet. He spoke quietly and with impressive conviction.

'Men, we're all beating around the bush

like hell. Why not come right into the open and make the proper move? Let's follow the lead the Bannister outfit has set and smoke the rest of the nesters out.'

This appeared to be a signal for all eyes to switch to Webb and his foreman. Across the table, Will Johnson had a cigar burning between his stubby fingers, and there was an expression on his face that could be interpreted as nothing but a sneer. As soon as Hollis sat down, Johnson rose and thumped the table with his fist.

'All right, gentlemen, it looks as if we're all in the same mind about this, so I figure the next step is to make some plans—'

Something drove Webb to push himself erect. Pete Hogan made a quick grab for his sleeve but Webb brushed the fingers away.

'Mr Chairman and gentlemen,' he began in a clear, incisive manner, 'I think we're overlooking something that should be given due attention. There is the small matter of procedure to be acknowledged, unless I've got the wrong end of the stick.'

'Procedure?' Will Johnson echoed, hard put to keep the scorn out of his tone. 'I'm afraid that Mr Bannister here is not accustomed to our ways of managing our affairs. What exactly do you mean by procedure?'

Webb could hear Pete Hogan groaning at his side. 'Well, I guess you could make it mean just about anything you want it to be. What I'm trying to get at is the fact that whatever decisions are made here tonight should be democratic decisions. And that calls for a vote.'

The word 'vote' had enough significance to produce a heavy silence that lasted for about ten seconds. Then Will Johnson smiled at Webb in a patronising way and nodded.

'A right good idea, Bannister. At least it'll let us see who's for us and who's against us.' He laughed shortly in a bogus attempt to rob the remark of malice. 'All right, friends, we'll run this level and above board as Mr Bannister suggests. He likely runs more cattle on this range than any of us, and his voice is one we ought to harken to.'

'Better pay attention to his fists as well, Will, unless I'm mistaken,' a grinning rancher suggested.

Johnson's brow darkened, but only for an instant. And now Webb could see that he really had heard about the fight in the saloon. Johnson thumped the table again, raised a hand.

'I'm going to propose that we hereby form our own association to stand vigilant and ready to act as we think necessary. With all due respects to the law here in Yellow Fork, you will agree with me that one man and a deputy are hardly adequate to keep the buzzards who prey on our herds at bay. So I propose that we swear here and now to get together and protect each other in our fight against the rogues and blackguards, to issue warning to them where necessary, and to drive them out. I propose, too, that we hang anyone we know to be a rustler...'

By then Webb was aware of a cold sweat forming on his brow. A sense of revulsion threatened to cut off his breathing. Pete Hogan noticed his agitation and placed a restraining hand on his knee.

'And now...' Johnson was saying dramatically, '...if everybody in favour will raise his hand we'll get this settled.'

Hands shot up all around the place. Webb was surprised when Pete signalled his agreement as well. Webb found himself going hot and cold. He could feel the weight of Will Johnson's burning stare on him.

'I don't see your hand in the air, Mr Bannister.'

'It's a free vote,' Webb replied flatly. 'I just don't happen to go along with it.'

'Webb, you damn fool!' Hogan groaned.

'Shut up, Pete. I don't think this is the right way to go about things.' He rose, feeling the heavy, accusing stares of the others in the room. 'Gentlemen, I'm sorry I can't agree with you. It's the reason I asked for a vote.'

'You'd better think again, mister,' somebody at the back of the room warned.

'I don't need to. The law is the law, but forming any kind of an association that takes the law into its own hands makes a mockery of justice. I'm sorry, but I can't agree with you.'

A low murmur ran over the gathering. Will Johnson cut it short by bringing his fist slamming down on the table yet again. There was a smugness about him now and a glint of triumph shone in his eyes.

'A man is entitled to his own opinion, I reckon,' he said tersely. 'And there might be circumstances here that we don't understand.'

'Horse dung!' somebody spat. 'Either he's in or he's out. And that means he don't deserve any protection.'

'I know how to look after myself,' Webb told them. Johnson's insinuation had not been lost on him, and he knew that here was a man he had better watch. He straightened his hat, turned to the door. 'Good night,' he said. 'Coming, Pete?'

'I'm damned if I am,' Hogan replied. 'I've had you up to here, Mr Bannister, sir. I'm quitting, and this time I mean it.'

'Suit yourself, Pete. You can collect your pay any time you wish.'

And so saying, Webb went on out and slammed the door behind him.

SEVEN

Outside, the main bar-room of the Buffalo Head was packed with cowhands awaiting the outcome of the meeting. The long counter was jammed with drinkers. Card games were in progress. Sheriff Buff Kane hovered around the batwing doors as if he couldn't quite make up his mind whether to stay or go into the street. Kane was accompanied by a skinny, nondescript character whom Webb took to be his deputy.

A hand reached out and touched Webb's arm. 'Meeting over, Bannister?'

Webb merely grunted and by-passed the fellow. He needed a drink, and elbowed in at the far end of the counter where he ordered a whiskey. He was sipping it when the other ranchers spewed out of the back room. Voices rose to a higher pitch now, excited, curious, demanding.

Webb watched the sheriff draw Will Johnson aside, where they talked for a minute. Johnson had a paleness about him as he pulled away. Buff Kane looked angry and spoke after him, but Johnson made a dismissive gesture with his hand. He stopped with no one else and headed on to the street.

Webb's restless gaze sought Pete Hogan now, found him. The foreman's eyes happened to touch him on the same instant and he immediately shouldered through the crowd to join Webb. He was breathing heavily.

'I want you to listen to me, boy. You've made a damn bad mistake, but there's still time to make good. These ranchers are your friends, and believe me, mister, you sure need all the friends you can get on this range.'

'Johnson for a friend!' Webb scoffed. 'Don't delude yourself, Pete. The only friend Will Johnson acknowledges is himself. He's number one and number two and number three. Get me?'

'All right, all right. I know how you feel. You're sore because his boys picked a fight with you. Everybody knows that Will is a tough old rooster. But don't forget that he started from nothing. He worked like hell to get what he has. You expect him to let every buzzard that comes along grab what he likes?'

'I understand all that, Pete. So he clawed his way up a pile of rocks and planted his flag on the top? But that doesn't give him the right to act as judge, jury and hangman.'

'What else can he do?' Hogan reasoned. 'You know the sort of riff-raff that's running around. They need their tails trimmed. So all right, we'll trim their tails. Now, listen, Webb, I told Johnson and Smith and the rest of them that I'd talk to you, try and make you see–'

'Save your breath, Pete,' Webb interrupted him.

'Do you know what's liable to happen unless you change your tune?' the older man rasped grimly.

'I've got a rough idea. I'll lose my ramrod for a start. And I'll really earn the tag of nester-lover.'

'You've only mentioned the half of it, boy. You could get the Indian sign put on you as well as the nesters. Think about it.'

'Then I'll just have to do something about

it, won't I?' Webb's tone was becoming ragged with anger.

Hogan swore in frustration. 'If the Old Man was alive he'd make you see things different. He'd make you see things the way they are.'

'He's not alive, Pete,' Webb came back testily. 'I'm in charge of Triangle B. I intend to run the outfit as I see fit. And no matter what you or anyone else says, I won't join any murdering band.'

Hogan made a gesture of defeat. His boney, teak-like face took on an expression of sympathy and caring. 'I'm sorry for you, boy. I really am.'

'Thanks for the kind thought, Pete. At least I'll have your good wishes even if I'm to be deprived of your services.'

The foreman ordered a whiskey and swallowed it in a gulp. He patted Webb's shoulder. 'Don't take any wooden nickels.'

Webb let a few seconds go by before turning to watch him shove his way through the crowd. Outside, the main street was noisy. Horses clattered about, whistled, pawed nervously. Men were talking loudly, laughing, as if, having failed to convince themselves, they were trying to convince others that everything would pan out all right.

Webb drank a beer and left the saloon. He had halted on the sidewalk when a tall figure shifted towards him out of the darkness. He recognized the heavily-built figure of Buff Kane and relaxed. He was slightly surprised to discover that the fingers of his right hand had been closing on the butt of his Colt.

'Mr Bannister?'

'Hello, Sheriff. Yellow Fork is certainly booming tonight.' He grinned and was rewarded with a snort of disgust.

'Any of your boys in town with you?' Kane wanted to know.

'Just my foreman. Didn't see much point in bringing any of the crew along.'

'Good idea. Why these half-smoked rannies have to make a night out of it is beyond me. I've been telling the ranchers to gather up their men and clear off home. I've already persuaded the farmers to leave town. It beats me why they can't all live and let live.'

'Do you think there'll be more trouble now, Sheriff?'

'What do you think?' the other growled. 'But I can tell you one thing for certain, mister: the first man that figures he can rod the law better than me is going to get a big surprise ... I believe you didn't go along with this vigilante notion?'

Webb tried to read his face in the gloom. It was hard trying to judge what Kane thought of him. 'Talk gets around this burg, doesn't it?' he said in non-committal fashion.

'Sure does. Well, I'd better mosey along. Good night, Mr Bannister.'

'Good night, Sheriff.'

Webb watched him until he had melted back into the darkness. He heard someone protest angrily, then the sheriff's voice lifted, high-pitched and authoritative. A horse broke away into the road. A bedlam of other noises rushed in. Webb rolled a cigarette, lighted it, deciding to get his own horse.

The livery was located in a side street that ran off an intersection, and he bent his steps towards it. Small groups of men still hung around in the shadows; others were making for the hitching posts and racks to collect their mounts. A storm of hoofbeats rolled down the road, raising clouds of dust. Webb flung his cigarette from him and quickened his pace, anxious now to get out of town and back to the ranch. He was aware of a sourness on his tongue, of an odd coiling in his stomach. The long ride home might help restore his equilibrium.

He was going past an alleyway when he glimpsed a shadowy figure drifting towards him. Instinct caused him to duck, but not fast enough. Something hard slammed down on the base of his neck and sent him sprawling in the dirt.

His senses reeled; lights blazed and died in his brain. He tried desperately to overcome the pain and its paralysing effects. He managed to raise himself to his knees. Then hands appeared to be clutching at him from every side. His arms were caught and twisted behind his back. He struggled and heaved, hearing a hoarse panting of breath that mingled with the noise issuing from his own throat, getting a raw reek of whiskey fumes in his face.

Something plunged into his stomach and he doubled over. A fist connected with the side of his face, rocking his head and threatening to tear it from his body. He was released suddenly and heard booted feet scattering in different directions. Then there was a space of silence when all he could hear was a thunderous agony bursting along his bloodstream. Footsteps were drawing near to him again. They were coming back to finish him off, he decided. And the merry hell of it was he could do nothing about it.

He clawed at the alley filth, thinking to push himself to his feet and get away before they caught him again.

A toe worked against his ribs, none too gently. 'What have we got here now, eh? Another baby with too much booze in his gut? Get up, mister, and make tracks before I make you drink something worse in the hoosegow. Up! Up!'

Webb groaned and tried to make his lips form words. Talking used to be so simple. No effort needed at all. It was something everybody did with the greatest of ease. They started wars with their mouths, caused murder. But he found that his lips were sealed now, as he might have said in a fit of whimsy.

A hand fastened on his shoulder and contrived to make him roll over on to his back. A lucifer sprang to life and filled the dark cavern of hell with forbidden light. There was a coarse ejaculation, an oath maybe. Join the happy band. The light went out.

'Holy cow, if it ain't Webb Bannister! Here you... Don't just stand and stare, dammit. Come over here and give Sheriff Buff Kane a helping hand. Yeah? What in hell are you scared of? There's a man hurt, you lunkhead.'

The next thing he knew was being laid down on something not so soft, but not so hard either. He was sprawled on a chair in the sheriff's office and Buff Kane's deputy was here, George Noonan. There was also a slim, elderly man present, and he was snapping a black leather bag shut. The bag was the traditional trademark of the cowtown sawbones.

Then Webb spotted Pete Hogan and wished the ground would swallow either him or his foreman.

'He'll live,' the medico declared. Then, louder, and with a forced smile, 'Hope you're feeling better, Mr Banning.'

'I'm fine, Doctor.'

The medico must have gone away, because Webb became aware of the sheriff looking into his face and asking him if he could remember what had happened.

'I was heading to the livery to collect my horse when somebody came at me from an alley. Maybe more than one. Three or four, possibly.' He tried to stand upright, and although Hogan would have supported him, he brushed Pete aside. A streak of pain lanced along his neck and he winced, touching the spot gingerly. 'They sure meant business, whoever they were.'

'Take your pick,' Pete Hogan said bitingly. 'You made more enemies tonight than an ordinary man would make in a lifetime. Got any ideas of your own?'

'Maybe Johnson's boys,' Webb suggested. 'On account of the Red Steer fracas.'

'Maybe,' Hogan grunted. 'Or a couple of ranchers who have learnt how to hate your guts. Another thing, Boss, you're making one hell of a reputation for yourself as a lion-tamer. How do you plan to live up to it?'

'I'll manage, I guess. Mind if I cut along, Sheriff?'

Buff Kane was poking at a tooth. He shook his head, and it was difficult to tell what he was thinking. 'Go right ahead if you're up to it. But steer clear of dark alleys and gents with clubs.'

'You bet. So long.'

Pete Hogan followed him into the dark street. There was a small crowd of curiosity-seekers around the doorway, and Hogan took over the lead, brushing the shadowy figures aside to let Webb through. Once clear, they went along the sidewalk together, Webb halting occasionally and Pete simply waiting for him to pull himself together and continue.

When they reached a gloomy intersection Webb looked around him. 'I believe it was some of Johnson's boys.'

'What's the difference?' Hogan snapped tartly. 'In my book, one enemy's much the same as another.'

'You moving over to their side, Pete?'

'Who said I was?' the foreman snarled. 'What do you take me for – a rat that just turns when it's cornered? You might be a hell of a lot of things I just can't figure out, but you're the Old Man's whelp, and he'd turn in his grave if I didn't look after you. But here, Webb ... there's something you'd better know. That Parker family's right here in Yellow Fork.'

Webb rocked to a halt at that, drawing a hard breath, fingering his neck and wishing the thumping in his head would ease up a little.

'Where – where are they?'

'Now, look, Boss, I only told you in case you got to worrying over the gal. I just heard that somebody saw them. I don't know where they're staying. What does it matter anyhow?'

Webb edged away. 'Thanks, Pete. I'll see you later.'

'But damn it, boy, you can't go around Yellow Fork on your own – especially tonight.'

'Sorry to spoil your plans,' Webb apologized with a weak grin. 'I don't know how you put up with me. I truly don't!'

Hogan sighed. 'This is the end of Triangle B,' he predicted dismally. 'The Old Man would never look me in the face again.'

'The Old Man had more sense than you give him credit for, maybe. You might have known a heap about my father, but you never heard it all, you bet.'

'What in hell are you talking about? Everybody's entitled to at least one skeleton in a cupboard.'

'My mother, old friend... Know something? My mother was the daughter of a medicine man. You know the gents who tote that cure-all poison around in their wagons. I'd say they kill more people than they cure. Well, sir, the said Mrs Coral Bannister used to fill the bottles with the coloured water her dad brewed over mesquite fires.'

That took Hogan under the belt right enough, but it would need a lot more to shake his faith in the Old Man. The Old Man had moved on from being an institution to being a legend, and you just didn't thumb your nose at legends unless you wanted to be struck down by a lightning bolt.

'What are you trying to say, damn you?' the foreman grated.

'Nothing much. But I want you to ride on home and leave me here. I'll be back at the ranch in two or three hours.'

'I'm going nowhere until you're good and ready to leave,' was the testy response. 'And arguing won't do you a damn bit of good.'

'Very well then. Keep making an occasional check at the livery stable.' Webb left Pete at that. He staggered a little for a while, but then he appeared to get his legs planted firmly beneath him. The crowd on the street was thinning somewhat and he went warily until he was at the front of the law-office once more. Buff Kane wasn't there, and the deputy's brows arched when the visitor inquired the way to the poorer quarter of Yellow Fork. The Parkers' financial situation wouldn't stretch to high-class hotels, and Josh would have to find lodgings to suit the weight of his purse.

'Klamath Street, in the south end,' George Noonan informed him. 'There's some old shacks that nobody owns. Nothing much but rats living in them these days. Say, are you looking for the gents who beat you up?'

'Nothing like that,' Webb assured him. He bade Noonan good night and left. Pete Hogan was waiting for him in the shadows.

'Come on and I'll show you the way,' he suggested in a resigned tone. 'But I still say you're loco, and if it gets around that you're soft on these nesters...'

'Everybody knows I love them all like brothers and sisters,' Webb flung back sourly. 'Let's go.'

They walked to the south end of town together, saying nothing to each other on the way. Klamath Street was a black alley, sour-smelling, totally uninviting.

'If they don't clear this part of town soon there'll be a fire that could wipe out everything,' Hogan predicted. 'Seriously, Webb, I just can't see anybody living in here.'

'I'll nose around all the same, Pete. Thanks again. See you later.'

He went on into the rutted street, peering all around him. When he glanced back, Hogan had disappeared. But you could ask a man to do only so much for you.

A hungry dog lurched out of the murk and tried to make a meal of his legs. Webb kicked it soundly and sent it tearing off, squealing furiously. He fancied he saw a glimmer of light behind a boarded window and went over to rap the door.

It was a long time before there was any response, then: 'Yeah, what you want, mister? Don't you know the time it is? Girls need a rest as well as anybody else.'

'Forget it.' He turned away, feeling sore, dispirited, and sorrier for the girls back there than he had ever known he could be.

He searched the miserable area from end

to end, several times risking being bitten by dogs that were just bound to be rabid. He went back on to Main and began making inquiries, discreetly at first, but then quite openly, as he could hardly bear the thought of Maureen Parker having to put up with any sort of privation. An hour later he heard that some travellers had camped a mile off the stage road, on the eastern outskirts of Yellow Fork. It was enough to send Webb to the livery where he saddled the grulla and took the stage route. He hadn't travelled far when he spotted a glow that might well mark a camp-fire.

He approached the site cautiously. His head still pounded and his muscles ached. More than anything else, he needed a long soak in a hot tub, with perhaps a bottle of whiskey beside him.

When he was really close to the ring of light shed by the fire-glow he brought his revolver from its holster. 'Hello, the camp!'

He started when a voice cut in from the shadows on his left. 'Hello yourself, mister. What do you want?'

'That you, Josh?'

'I'll be damned if it ain't that Bannister galoot!' Josh Parker erupted excitedly. 'Ride on in, fella, but none of your funny tricks.

Seems you can be trickier than a sackful of monkeys.'

When he edged in closer to the fire Webb saw the outline of a tent, the shafts of a wagon. Beyond, cattle shifted restlessly, lowed complaint, as well they might. He watched as a figure stepped out of the tent. He ran his tongue over his lips, dismounted carefully.

'Webb...'

'Howdy, Maureen,' he drawled, trying to quell the hard thumping of his heart at sight of her again.

She came right up to him and peered into his face. 'What – what do you want? Why are you following us around?'

'For the best reason in the world,' he answered huskily. 'I wanted to see you again.'

He thought she might have slapped his face, if only to ease the terrible agony of frustration she must feel; she could have been forgiven for bawling him out. But some flash of intuition caused him to let his arms fall apart, then form a loose, inviting circle. And, just as intuitively, the girl knew there was only one possible way she could react. She moved into the circle and allowed it to close around her protectively.

Webb touched her forehead with his lips.

'Maureen.' It was a low groan.

'No!' she protested when the enormity of the situation hit her. 'You're mad, Webb. You can't–'

'Oh, yes, I can. Everybody says I'm loco. Everybody figures I'm just about the worst cowman ever to straddle leather. But I don't care what they think.'

Parker, in the meantime, had managed to get closer to them, and now he yelled at the visitor. 'Damn you for a sneaky coyote, Bannister! If you don't back off from my girl I'm gonna let a chunk of lead clear through your backbone. Reen, get away from him.'

'You'll have to shoot me as well, Dad,' his daughter informed him. 'Webb isn't doing anything I don't want him to do.'

'You're crazy, honey. What this jasper needs is a bullet under his tail.'

Webb drew away from the girl and looked over at the tent. 'Where's Jim?'

'He got on his horse right after the Lazy J men ran us off our site,' Parker supplied. 'He wasn't as badly hurt as we figured.'

Webb reached a decision. 'Listen, Josh, you and Maureen are coming into Yellow Fork with me. There's a passable hotel where you can stay until it's safe to go ahead with your homestead plans. And your best plan would be to file on open land. Take a quarter-section and prove up on it. Squatters' rights will–'

Parker's derisive laugh interrupted him. 'Hotel sounds mighty fine, Mr Bannister, but I've only got a small stake, in case you don't know.'

'You won't have to worry about paying the bill.'

'Charity!' the other exploded. 'Mister, I don't rightly cotton to your game, but if you don't back up quick you're in trouble.'

'Take it easy, I'm not offering charity. Anything I do for you can be repaid when you get your place going. Or maybe you don't have enough faith in yourself to go out on a limb that far?' Webb added tartly.

The old-timer drew a hand across his mouth and Webb detected a quick glimmer of hope in his eyes. But then Parker shook his head.

'Sorry, Mr Bannister. You're acting like a square gent: there's no denying that. But I figure you might be doing this to bluff Reen.'

Webb stifled a curse. 'If you weren't such an old coot I'd push that right back into your teeth,' he growled. 'Maureen, would you try talking sense to him?'

148

Parker stalked away into the darkness and the girl looked into Webb's face. 'I – I don't know what to say,' she panted, 'what to do...'

'Do you trust me?' he demanded bluntly.

'Oh, if I only could! But you must understand, Webb. We've been pushed around so much that I think I might have lost faith in human nature. If only Dad had stayed on his farm when my mother died things might have worked out differently. But he grew so restless, dissatisfied with his life. And he soon used up all his money...'

'I understand. But I'm going to ask you to trust me, Maureen. Will you do that?'

She began sobbing afresh and he brought her into his arms again. For a long time they were oblivious to everything around them.

Then Parker shouted brusquely from the shadows. 'Hey, Bannister, if you really figure to help, give me a hand to load the wagon. But if I'm putting my shirt on a loser horse it'll be a dead nag when the race is over.'

EIGHT

For a week Webb devoted most of his energies to the affairs of the ranch. Things were quiet enough on the range, but his riders kept bringing reports that Will Johnson's men were displaying unusual zeal in the way they were throwing Triangle B cattle back when they drifted on to Lazy J land.

There was a fracas of sorts, too, when Bill Sloan and a Johnson rider met beyond the creek ford and words were bandied. The subject of nesters had been brought up and Sloan had warned the Lazy J man to swallow his guff or suffer the consequences. An out-and-out fight had been averted by the intervention of Pete Hogan. Seen from a detached view-point, it was little more than a ripple on a wide enough pond, and Webb was reluctant to attach any great importance to it.

His foreman did not share his opinion. 'I happen to know Will Johnson better than you do,' he advised Webb. 'He can be a good friend, but a devilish bad enemy.'

'I'm not tramping on his toes, Pete. As

long as he minds his own business, I'll mind mine.'

'Let's hope it stays like that,' the other declared darkly.

His foreman's manner towards him had undergone a subtle change since the ranchers' meeting in Yellow Fork. Where hitherto Hogan had been cool with Webb on occasions, and at times even openly hostile, Pete now showed a desire to please his boss in all aspects of the ranch workings. Webb wondered if the change was due to the fight in the Red Steer. He wondered, also, if Pete was simply putting up a front to hide his true feelings, which might not have altered one iota.

So far, Pete had made no mention of the Parker family again; he had not even inquired if Webb had succeeded in finding the Parkers that night. His silence in this respect irked Webb for a while, but he finally decided to accept the situation as it stood.

Towards the end of the week he had a visit from Sheriff Buff Kane and his deputy, George Noonan. He had learnt in the meantime that the sheriff's given name was Clarence, and the nickname had sprung from some long-ago buffalo story, about which no one was clear.

Kane didn't stay long. Ostensibly, he was just 'looking around' and 'trying to get a picture of things'. He explained that there had been another raid by rustlers on a ranch owned by Breck Hollis up north. It wasn't looking very good, was it? 'And if I don't come up with some results soon, these ranchers are liable to do something damn stupid, like taking the law into their own hands.'

'That would be the worst move they could make,' Webb declared.

Buff Kane regarded him from under half-closed eyelids. 'You're a queer bird, Mr Bannister. Not much like your father, are you?'

Webb shrugged. 'I don't have to be.' He wondered what Kane was driving at. Then he thought of the Parkers and felt heat crawling up his neck and into his face. The lawman noticed and grinned.

'I heard what might just be a rumour, Mr Bannister. Correct me if I've got it wrong. You're looking after a nester family in town?'

'That's my affair,' Webb came back curtly.

'Sure it is! Don't get me wrong. I'm all for helping my weary brother to carry his burden. But what will your neighbours think?'

'I don't pay much attention to what they think.'

'Well, what about that now!' The eyes

opened wide, glinted. 'I wish there were more folks in these parts with your sort of spirit, mister.'

'Would you like to stay and have a meal with us, Sheriff?'

'No, thanks, Bannister. See you around.'

Kane and the eagle-eyed, taciturn Noonan were on the point of leaving, and the sheriff was lighting a stogie before he went, when another thought seemed to occur to him. 'Oh, yes, I nearly forgot. That brother of the girl's... He ain't in town, is he?'

'I know nothing about Jim Parker, Sheriff.'

'No, no, of course you don't. Well, so long for now.'

Webb was thoughtful as he watched them ride off. So it had already got around that he had put the Parkers up in a hotel in town? A story like that would spread far and fast. It would become warped in the telling, naturally. It would, of course, acquire dark connotations that would be discussed with sly relish in saloon bar-rooms. He realized that Pete Hogan must have heard as well, and likely that was why Pete was keeping quiet about the Parkers.

He swore softly. It was beginning to look as if Hogan was deliberately throwing him enough rope to hang himself, and when he was well and truly tangled, Pete could stand back and claim smugly: 'I told you so.'

Saturday morning brought news of another incident that increased the tension. Will Johnson and four of his men clattered into the front yard soon after sun-up. They had ridden hard and far, judging by their appearance, and Johnson sprang from his horse to confront Webb and his foreman. The rancher's eyes were bleak as they ran past the Triangle B boss to the stocky Hogan.

'Pete, we lost more stuff last night,' he said raggedly. 'The boys managed to break up the rustlers, and a couple of them were seen loping out in this direction.'

'Ain't seen nobody, Will,' the foreman responded. 'But I'll have a word with the nighthawks as soon as they come in.'

'That'll be too late,' the cowman snorted. He passed a big hand over his gun leather. 'But we'll get them sooner or later. Skeeter Flynn got a look at one of them and he swears it was that Parker gent that was squatting at Silver Creek.'

'Ahuh! Well, they ain't there now, Will. We chased them out.'

'Heard you did, Pete. But you know something? I hear they're nicely fixed up in a hotel in town. Pretty good going for dirt-farmers, you'd say?'

Pete Hogan bit his underlip and nodded. Johnson's eyes were back on Webb at this juncture, bright with accusation. Webb swallowed thickly but said nothing.

Johnson coughed and spat. 'You haven't seen this Parker fella, Mr Bannister?' he queried slowly.

'Last time I saw him he was on your land,' Webb answered. 'With a bullet in his hide.'

'Pity the bullet didn't do what it was supposed to do. But he'll have a lot of trouble wriggling out of a noose.'

'You've got a right to your opinions and convictions, Johnson.'

'Too true I have! And that means you've got a right to yours.'

'He has, Will,' Pete Hogan interjected coolly.

'Pete, I always had you figured as a man with a grain of know-how. I hope you haven't lost your senses.'

'Not so you'd notice. We done told you, Will,' Hogan added testily. 'We ain't seen your rustlers.'

It was a plain hint that the Triangle B men had said all they intended saying for the time being. Johnson's face went very white and he lifted himself into his saddle. Settled in leather, his right hand swept along his thigh, touching the walnut stock of the thonged-down Colt .45.

'Just because a nester hides in a cowman's town doesn't say he's safe,' he announced with dark meaning for Webb.

'So long, Johnson,' Webb said thinly.

'Don't worry, Bannister, I'm going. But I might be back.'

'There'll always be somebody here to welcome you,' was Webb's stony rejoinder.

The Lazy J men rode off and Hogan moved away from the dust they stirred up. 'Trouble,' he growled. 'I can smell it coming.'

'He's trying to ride me, Pete. I watched his face at the meeting. He really wanted me to go against the rest. I could see him gloating when I made my stand.'

'That figures. And it was likely some of his boys who roughed you up after the meeting. He's a mean old rooster when he's roused.'

'He can't hurt me,' Webb said as if speaking to himself. 'He can try, but it won't work.'

Hogan's eyes held mild scorn. 'You ought to know by now whether he can hurt you. Supposing he tries to take it out on the Parkers for that Jim galoot?'

Webb paled at the suggestion. 'Pete, he wouldn't–'

'He might. Listen, boy, I don't aim to butt into your private affairs. But this gal... What does she mean to you?'

Webb hesitated for only a moment before answering. 'I think a whole lot of her. Maybe more than you imagine. I might marry her if she'll have me.'

The foreman whistled softly. 'You do tell! I didn't know it was like that. I was beginning to wonder what sort of coyote you were, keeping that gal stashed away in the hotel. You know what folks might wonder?'

'It didn't occur to me at the beginning, but I'm beginning to realize what they might wonder.' Webb grinned. 'I guess I am a tenderfoot in some ways, Pete.'

'Not in the way that matters,' the other assured him. 'So that's settled then. Well, I don't give a damn about Johnson now, nor the others either. But this brother...'

'He's got a wild streak in him.'

'Sure. And it'll be a pity if it takes one of Johnson's ropes to cure his wildness,' was the foreman's grim rejoinder.

On Saturday nights, most of the crew usually hit out for Yellow Fork, and at sundown Webb got Jed to saddle up the sorrel and took the trail with Pete Hogan. Hogan warned him to stay away from any cowhands who might try dragging him into a row, and Webb assured him that getting into another fight was the last thing on his mind.

On arrival in town, they turned their horses in at the livery. Then Webb joined Pete in the Buffalo Head for a couple of beers. Afterwards, Hogan spotted a couple of old cronies he hadn't seen in a long time and joined them, with a final injunction to his boss to watch his step.

The main street of the town bustled with life, and Webb lingered on the sidewalk to light a cigar and allow the relaxed atmosphere to ease the tensions that rode him. There was always a chance that some outfit might pick on his crew – Lazy J in particular. Where, before, the two outfits had been on friendly enough terms, there now existed a condition of impending strife that could well erupt into an outright feud.

After a while Webb found his steps wending towards the hotel where the Parkers were located. He asked the desk clerk if Miss Parker was in her suite and learned that she was. The clerk was conversant with the circumstances leading to the Parkers being lodged here, but he showed no animosity towards the Triangle B boss.

'Reckon you'd like to go up by yourself, Mr Bannister?'

'Thanks pard. If you don't mind.'

He climbed the stairs and made his way along the narrow corridor until he reached the last door on his right. He tapped with his knuckles and soon heard a voice. 'Yes, who is it?'

'*Hombre* by the name of Bannister, Miss Parker.'

'Webb!'

The door was drawn open and Maureen Parker rushed into his arms. He held her close, savouring the warmth of her, the sheer animal softness of her body, letting some heady scent drown his senses. When she turned her face to him he kissed her on the mouth, tenderly, for all the hunger that gnawed at him. He had come here with a decision made and he was impatient to state it.

They broke apart and she led him into the room. He glanced around him, looking for Josh.

'Where's your dad?'

She sank down on a sofa and he sat beside her, frowning at the tears he saw forming in her eyes. 'Webb, I – I'm so worried. Dad heard some rumours about Jim. They said the sheriff was hunting for him. Some rancher reported seeing Jim with rustlers.'

Webb swallowed tightly. This damn brother needed a stern lesson. 'But what about your father? Where is he?'

'He's gone to look for Jim. I – I don't know where. He believes that unless he finds him and gets him to see sense, something awful will happen to him. The ranchers have formed a vigilante committee and they'll kill anyone they find near their cattle. I blame that man Singleton McCall. He – he can wrap Jim around his little finger.'

Webb stood up. 'How long since your dad left?'

'A day. He rode out yesterday morning. We managed to sell our stock to one of the butchers. He just kept his horse. Webb, if – if anything happened to Dad, I don't know what I'd do.'

It was on Webb's lips to state the nature of his visit, but he held the words back. Perhaps this was not the best time to speak.

'Have you been comfortable here?' he asked, trying to take her thoughts away from her father and brother.

'Everything's fine. And everyone has been

so kind to us, but–' She broke off to stare at him, her eyes wide, her cheeks suffused with colour.

Webb grinned. 'This isn't exactly the wild-cat I found out at Silver Creek. Say, remember how you were going to tear me apart?'

Her colour deepened and she dropped her head. Webb placed a finger under her chin and raised it again. Her eyes were misted with tears.

'Everything has changed,' she said huskily. 'Since, since...'

'Since I fished your dress out of the creek,' he murmured. 'Look, Maureen, I want to–'

Heavy footsteps sounded outside in the corridor. Then the door was opened without ceremony and Josh Parker stepped into the room.

'Dad!' The girl dashed to him, gripped his arms. Parker looked weary, defeated. He dipped his head briefly to Webb, sank down on a chair and pushed his hat up from his steamy brow.

'Golly, I haven't done so much riding in years. Webb, you haven't heard anything about Jim at all?'

'Dad, you mean you didn't find him?'

'Not a sign, honey.'

Webb recalled what Will Johnson had told

him that morning. He decided to keep it to himself. He lifted his hat, drew it on. Maureen was immediately concerned.

'You're not leaving so soon?'

'Yes, I've got to drift. I'll keep an eye out for Jim.'

'If you find him, try and get some sense into his thick head,' Parker said with a sigh of desperation. 'Oh, before you go, Bannister, I've been looking at a neat little place...'

'That's good. But I'd advise you to hold your hand for a while, Josh. At least until this rustling scare has died down.'

'But we can't stay here in style and let you foot the bill,' the other protested. 'I've got my pride, mister, and it sure goes against my grain to sit around here, twiddling my thumbs.'

'Forget it. You'll just have to work harder to pay me back when you get started. And maybe one of these days I'll be asking you a favour,' he added with a glint in his eye.

'Anything, boy! All you have to do is mention it. Anything!'

Webb dare not look at Maureen as he backed to the door. 'See you soon, folks,' he said breezily and ducked out.

He was thoughtful as he went down the stairs to the lobby. The clerk raised a hand

and hurried out from behind his desk. 'Just a minute, Mr Bannister,' he said anxiously. 'Stay where you are.'

'Hey, what's biting you? Didn't I settle–'

'Don't go into the street. Heard some men talking about you. They've been drinking plenty and they're armed to the teeth. Look, you could slip out the back way. Let me show you.'

A chill had entered Webb's bloodstream. 'Know who they are? Lazy J boys?'

'Can't say for sure, Mr Bannister. But I know they're set for you. Why risk getting hurt? Come on out back.'

'Slink off like a frightened coyote? Thanks, friend, but that's one habit I haven't mastered yet.'

'Then by heaven you'd better get ready for fireworks,' the other warned. Sweat shone on his brow as Webb went on to the street door.

He paused on the hotel gallery until his eyes became accustomed to the gloom. He glimpsed a figure a couple of yards but from the sidewalk; he soon recognized him and caught his breath. Where were the others?

Skeeter Flynn sniggered when he spotted him. 'So you've been calling on your lady love, Mr Bannister?' Flynn drawled sardonically. 'Just goes to show what a dirty renegade you are.'

Webb said nothing, just concentrated on combing the shadows for the others. There just had to be others. Flynn was merely the worm on the hook. He felt his muscles bunching in eagerness, his nerves tensing.

'Did you hear what I said, Bannister?' Flynn thundered now. When he lifted his voice like that he gave himself away. He had a lot of drink under his belt and his nerve wasn't nearly as firm as he would have Webb believe.

'Who could help hearing you, Flynn?' Webb replied equably. 'Now, why don't you take a word of advice and stop acting the fool? You've already made your play and lost. I don't want any more trouble with you.'

'I just bet you don't! But you're going to get it all the same, fella. Let's see if you're as slick with your shooting iron. *Draw!*'

There was no time to consider, no time to argue the point. Skeeter Flynn's hand was driving furiously for his revolver before the last word had left his lips.

His first shot made a tremendous bang and the bullet hummed wickedly past Webb's head and crashed through the window of the hotel lobby. Then Webb had his own Colt clear and was working the trigger coolly, calmly, the way the old gunslinger friend he had known had taught him.

He saw Flynn spring up on his heels, saw the gout of flame that lanced at him again. More bullets thudded into the hotel brickwork. The clerk yelled. Flynn appeared to lose all interest in trying to fly and, instead, crumpled at the knees before tilting over on his face.

But that wasn't the whole of it. No sooner had these thunderclaps died than another revolver took up the challenge. Bullets whined and sang past Webb's head and body like a swarm of hornets. He went to his knees at the back of a roof support and triggered until his revolver was empty. He hugged the foul-smelling duckboards while he re-loaded. There was a temptation to do this in a frenzy, but he forced himself to be cool, schooled his actions so that they were delib-erate. *Thank you Mark Greenwood, for your schooling in the gentlemanly art of shooting the hell out of a bunch of cowardly bastards... Sorry, Maureen, I didn't mean to be so uncouth, so brutal. I'm really a very nice fellow at heart. But not just now... Just now it's kill or be killed...*

He finished re-loading, snapped the gate, glimpsed someone racing for the opposite side of the street. The man fired over his shoulder, declaring him for one of the enemy, so Webb let him have a single round. He must have missed. The man vanished. But now there was another one working his way down the plankwalk from the corner of the hotel. He aimed and fired, then broke into a run in the other direction.

Webb reached the end of the plankwalk and stumbled in the drop-off to the alley. He righted himself and moved the gun in a slow, searching arc. There was a feral smile at his lips that he wasn't aware of, but his heart was thumping healthily and he could hardly believe that the laugh he heard was coming from his own throat.

On along the street there was a throng of people. There was much heated talking, shouting, questioning. Webb heard a hard step behind him and swung. Here was a third would-be killer, tall, rangy, gun swinging at his side. Webb sent a shot at him, then continued his weaving run.

He knew when he was at the front of a saloon, and dashed through the line of horses racked there. He ducked and made for the high batwing doors, thrust them inwards just as a blocky figure emerged.

'Webb, what the hell's going on?'

'Look out,' Webb warned Pete Hogan. 'That was some of the Lazy J outfit trying to bushwhack me.'

'I'll give them bushwhacking, damn them,' was the fierce rejoinder. 'Come on.'

Hogan joined him in the shadowy murk that clung to the shuttered stores and narrow alleyways. They put their backs to the wall of one of these stores and, revolvers fanning slowly, looked around them. It had gone strangely quiet.

'Where do you figure they're at?' Hogan wondered.

'Don't know.'

'Nail any of them?'

'Can't be sure. Say ... it's quiet.'

'There's the reason,' Hogan snorted. 'The law. Don't let Kane spot you. It'll be a sword to keep pointing at you. Come on!'

They melted away into one of the bigger pools of blackness. Had any of Will Johnson's men showed, they would have been blasted down where they stood. The Triangle B men gained the livery stable. They took time to regulate their breathing, and Webb found a cigar stub in his pocket. He proceeded to light up before going to take his horse out. They had almost finished saddling when heavy footsteps preceded the figure of Buff – or Clarence – Kane breaking into the pool of meagre lamplight, Kane battled with a hustling chest until he had enough air in his lungs to speak.

'Was that you fellas on the run just now?' he demanded while his hooded eyes snapped, first at Pete Hogan, and then at his boss.

'Reckon not, Sheriff,' Hogan replied coolly. 'No sir, Buff. Fact is, we heard some fireworks down the road yonder and decided it might be healthier on the trail home. Fellas like us can't afford to get mixed up in queer deals. What do you say, Boss?'

'Who, me?' Webb queried. 'Well, Pete, I think the sheriff knows I'm against violence in any shape or form. Isn't that so, Mr Kane?'

The lawman glared at the hostler standing in the doorway of his office, but as soon as he took a step towards him the stable-man went inside and closed the door behind him.

'All right, Mr Bannister,' Kane said softly after a long pause. 'I won't delay you. I know where I can always find you. Right, Mr Bannister? Right, Mr Hogan?'

'Sure thing, Buff,' Hogan agreed. Then, suppressing a laugh that persisted in gurgling up in his throat: 'All right, Boss, let's get away from this hell-raising burg before some of them gunslingers takes a shot at us.'

They rode out of town together and, when they were a couple of miles along the stage road, they halted to test the wind. There was nothing to be seen or heard, and they went on at a brisk pace. There were two important questions that Webb required answered: was Will Johnson bent on maiming him or killing him at the first opportunity? What would Jim Parker do now when he realized that the cowmen were hunting for him?

NINE

Pete Hogan spotted the red glow against the skyline before Webb did. They were about two miles from ranch headquarters, pulling up a long hill, when the foreman reined in and pointed.

'Hey, look yonder!'

Webb picked up the shimmer of light and swore in amazement. Grey mist swirled thickly, and the dampness of the earth was wafted to their nostrils. The horses, almost worn out, were forced into a punishing run.

Both men raced to the crest of a bare ridge, peered towards the site of the ranch-house once more. The glow had become a huge blob of crimson that hung like a monstrous curtain across the night.

All sorts of speculation and fears drummed through Webb's brain in a confused welter. Was that really the ranch-house on fire? How had it started? And then a vision of Will Johnson's sneering face rose in front of him and his mind became numb for a moment before fury rushed in like a searing brand.

Crawling closer to the front yard, he uttered a sob of relief when he saw the outlines of the main buildings intact. The fire was away from the house itself, at the rear. Gigantic plumes of sparks scattered against the heavens. The two men thundered into the yard and whirled on around the corner. Shadowy figures were darting hither and thither, hauling buckets of water, calling to each other. The fire was devouring the stable, and the screaming and whistling of fear-crazed horses told Webb that some of the stock were trapped in there.

He and Pete hit the ground at a run. Their horses spooked and Pete grabbed them and tethered them at the far side of the back yard. Webb hurried to join him. There were only three cowhands at home. What a night to start a fire!

Someone called raggedly, 'We've done our best, Boss. But it's got too big a hold.'

Webb stared at the seething mass. A wild threshing reached his ears, a sharp whistle of pure terror. 'The horses...'

'No chance of getting them,' Pete Hogan shouted. 'And don't you try.'

Webb paid no heed. He grabbed a bucket of water Jed was carrying, emptied it over his head and body. The roustabout swore fearfully.

'Never mind,' Webb flung at him. 'Just keep at it. Try and prevent it spreading.' He raised his right arm to shield his eyes, then ducked and pierced a solid sheet of flame. He heard someone shrill a warning that was soon drowned in the roar and crackle of burning timbers.

The interior of the stable was like a scalding oven, yet only two walls were really ablaze. Webb tried to breathe, and smoke-laden air choked him. His eyes stung and smarted. Tears blinded him. He heard a horse trying to kick itself free of a stall, reached the stall gate, and swung it open. The beast whirled and screamed, eyes rolling whitely. It lunged past him and ran towards the flames.

Webb went after it, slapping its rump, sidestepping the lashing hooves. The horse spun then and reared, and charged for the opening where the night air was fanning the furnace glow. Another beast was trapped in here, close to that high, raging wall. Webb tried to beat his way to it, and the hungry tongues of crimson licked at his clothing and skin until he was sure he would soon be nothing but a burning brand himself.

He dropped to the floor in an effort to drag air into his tortured lungs. He heard a rending tear, and sprang up just as the end wall began moving slowly but inexorably towards him.

His senses swam. He gritted his teeth and dashed aside, reached the stall where the frantic horse was kicking out. He was trying to shift the gate when someone grabbed his arm and roared in his ear.

'You damn fool... Come on!'

The wall had poised now; it started bending up near the top. The screaming of the horse filled his ears. He saw Pete Hogan limned against the glare. The gate went inwards and the horse bore around and sent the foreman on to his back. Part of the wall came at them. Heavy, flame-wrapped supports broke free with a mighty crackling and plunged to the ground.

Webb went down in a storm of bursting sparks and billowing smoke. He heard Pete calling hoarsely, rolled on to his face, and knew he was finished. When Pete bent over him like some grim monster out of Hades he pushed him away.

'Save yourself, I – can't – make it...'

'Get out, you lousy tenderfoot!' Hogan yelled.

He reached his knees, tried desperately to find a breath of air to soothe his scalding lungs. His legs moved without him really being aware of this. He never remembered exactly how he broke through the wall of crimson streaked with stark black and throbbing stains of smoke. All he knew was that there was glorious air and that his lungs were still functioning. He sucked greedily, knowing he would never get enough. Then the air appeared to be running into his lungs in a torrent that choked him and sent him into a fit of coughing. He could feel eager hands reaching for him, dragging him through the dirt and smoke. His clothes reeked, smouldered. As he watched, the torn left leg of his pants burst into flame.

Water hit him, bowled him into a constricted knot, gasping, rolling, shivering. He managed to make it to his feet, and was no sooner upright than he spun to launch himself at the stable once more.

'Pete,' he croaked. 'I've got to get Pete...'

'He's here, Boss. He's safe.'

They clutched him and held him back. And when he saw Pete Hogan on his haunches, retching violently, he shook himself loose, thankful that his foreman had reached safety.

There was little else that anyone could do after that. The fire was having its way, but would burn out without damaging the rest of the buildings. The men stood off now, watching in a stunned manner as the stable was finally reduced to a seething, smouldering hulk of ash and charred timber.

When Webb recovered somewhat he hunted for Jed, the roustabout. The old fellow sat with his back against a fire barrel. He was close to exhaustion and held a hand to his heaving chest. Webb waited for a few minutes before speaking, then asked Jed what had happened.

'Ain't rightly sure, Boss,' he wheezed. 'But it wasn't an accident. I can tell you that for sure. I was in time to hear them racing off.'

'When the fire started?'

'It was the noise that took me to the stable,' the old-timer explained. 'The fire was just getting under way. I admit I spooked for a minute, but then I gathered my wits and went to the bunkhouse. Dick and Slim were there, and they came on the trot. We just fetched buckets and went to work. At first I figured the whole place would go up.'

'You didn't see the horsemen?'

Jed shook his head. Pete Hogan had been squatting on his haunches a little distance off, smoking, listening. He pushed himself upright. His face was almost as black as the surrounding night.

'It's plain that firebugs caused it,' he contributed bitterly.

'But who? Who would do such a thing, Pete?'

'Any of the cowmen could have done it. You figure they're angels on horseback? Like blazes they are! They're imps out of hell when they want to be. And you know what's behind it, don't you? Maybe you should have joined them, Webb.'

'You think it was Johnson? Would he stoop to a trick like this?'

'It's hard to say. But you're in bad with them. Especially after shooting Skeeter Flynn.'

'Pete, I'm going to get a fresh horse and light out for Lazy J.'

'You really want to get yourself killed? It would be a crazy move.'

'I'm going. Jed, if you feel up to it, get me a horse out. The grulla, if it's handy. I'll be ready to ride in a minute.'

He headed for the house. There was a burn on his left leg that caused him to limp slightly. His face felt as if there was no skin left on it. His eyes still stung and watered. He had lost his hat in the fire, and he found another one on the buckhorn rack. He loaded his belt with shells, took a Winchester from its wall pegs, a weapon that had belonged to the Old Man. He wondered fleetingly what his father would have done in a situation like this. Would he have taken his time and sniffed around until he was sure he had picked up the right scent, or would he have done what his son intended doing?

There was no time to ponder. Webb considered getting out of his wet and stinking clothing: he looked like a neglected scarecrow. Instead, he drank about a quart of water and went into the night once more.

Pete Hogan was telling the men to stay alert in case the fire rekindled or threatened to spread. Webb didn't think it would. The foreman had two horses ready to ride and

Webb protested.

'Pete, you need a rest. Let me handle this on my own.'

'You could hardly find your way to Lazy J in the dark,' the other snorted. 'I'm going along.'

There was no point in arguing, and they set off together. In the saddle, Webb became aware of a host of other minor burns as they began to sting. He tried to disregard them, tried to forget the discomfort of damp, dirty clothing clinging to his skin. Pete was in pretty much the same state.

They had gone only a couple of miles, and were working through a section of brush and rocks when a rifle cracked away out on their left.

Webb rolled from his saddle, acting instinctively, kicking his boots free of the stirrups. By the time he hit the ground Pete was scrambling for the cover of a large boulder. The rifle snarled again and brush popped and shredded against Webb's face.

He saw the grulla mincing and threatening to dash off. He judged the distance to the horse, sprang upright, and ran towards it. The marksman blasted at him, and Hogan returned the fire.

Another weapon cut in as Webb reached

his mount and snapped his Winchester free of the scabbard. His boots slithered on loose shale as he made a dive for cover. He marked the spot where Pete Hogan was located and wormed his way towards it.

Gunfire fairly lashed the night, pocking the shadows with blobs of orange and deep crimson. Lead hissed and whined in quest of targets. Then Webb had reached Pete's side and immediately jacked a shell into the breech of the Winchester.

He waited until the ambushers in the rocks fired once more, then triggered into a gout of flame, ducking as a slug whined past his head. Pete took over, poking his gun barrel out. Then, as suddenly as the shooting had begun, it stopped, and Webb heard his own breathing rasping in time with the pumping of his heart.

'What are they up to?' he wondered.

'Hard to say,' Hogan whispered. 'They could be coyoting through the rocks up there.'

They waited and watched, and at length Webb rose to his feet, only to be hauled back under cover. 'Easy. They'd blow the head off your shoulders as quick as look at you.'

Pete had just finished speaking when they

heard hooves scraping and cracking on rock before picking up a rhythm of sorts. Hogan slapped his boss on the shoulder.

'They're pulling out. Come on.'

They lost precious minutes hunting around for their horses and getting mounted. Then Pete began working up through the jumble of rocks where the bushwhackers had been lying in wait. He was first through a ragged gap in the wild upheaval and Webb heard him utter a curse. He pushed his grulla forward and soon came on the foreman, stooped over the dark form of a man on the ground.

'One of the ambushers?'

'Sure looks like it.' Hogan scanned the cliffs that reared on all sides in case someone was watching them, with a rifle trained on them. 'Got a match?' he asked.

Webb struck a match, but the breeze caught the flame and killed it. He scratched another one, cupped it in his palms until Pete turned the man on to his back. In the feeble illumination they were able to make out a pain-ridden face. Webb remembered the squat man who had helped Singleton McCall beat him up at the Silver Creek location.

'It's one of the rustlers,' he said.

'Sure? I've never seen him in my life.'

'He was with McCall and another man when they gave me that hiding over on the south fork.'

'But you said you didn't know them,' Hogan accused. 'Now wait a minute...' Pete's tone hardened. 'Did you say that on account of Jim Parker being there?'

'Jim was wounded. He was in a tent.'

'Not now he ain't, boy. It's my bet he's riding with the wideloopers.'

He stopped speaking when the man on the ground muttered something. Webb scratched another match alight, held the flame shielded.

'What is it, friend?' Hogan queried. 'Who are you? Why were you trying to ambush us?'

'Basset... They – left me.'

'They sure did, bub. They plain hit out and left you to croak it. But we might be able to help if you tell us a few things. How about it?'

'I – uh – can't...'

'Sure you can. Look, I'll make it easy for you. Was that Singleton McCall you were hoofing around with?'

'No. That was ... Jim Parker. Wanted to get a crack at Webb Bannister, he said. Then they're – meeting Single and the others. Going to make a – big – steal...'

The voice dwindled off and the man gave a hoarse gasp. Webb saw him shudder violently before he went still. He bent over him and checked for pulse, then raised his head to his foreman.

'He's dead, Pete.'

'Playing possum, most likely,' Hogan snorted.

It turned out to be true. And when he saw that his subterfuge had failed, the rustler attempted to sit up. 'You said – you'd help me.'

'Sure will, pard,' Hogan responded breezily. 'Just as soon as you tell us where your friends are going to dab their loops.'

'Lazy J,' the other mouthed weakly. He made a sudden lunge at Webb who still hunkered beside him, grabbed the revolver from his holster before Webb had time to collect his wits. 'Damn you!' he panted, rolling back and attempting to cock the weapon.

Webb flung himself aside as Pete Hogan palmed his own six-shooter and triggered in a single, smooth motion. The bushwhacker screamed in agony, pitched over into the rocks, and hung there for a minute, struggling for breath, hurling invectives at the two cowmen. Then he stopped struggling and talking and his head fell forward.

'He's dead now,' Hogan said grimly. 'Never, never trust a sidewinder, son.'

Webb said nothing. He retrieved his Colt, found that the bandit had failed to ear back the hammer, restored it to its pouch.

'Thanks, Pete.'

'Forget it.'

'Lazy J?' Webb murmured then. 'So Jim Parker intends making a big night of it – trying to burn down our place, then lying up in ambush. He must be absolutely crazy, Pete.'

'Just plain crazy,' Hogan's mouth warped in a grin. 'He's riding high, and that means he's about to get a bad fall.'

'But why has he gone to the bad when – when his sister and father are such decent people?'

'Hell, I don't know. Maybe he was suckled by a wolf. But I'd say he resents you looking after his dad and sister. He and his friends aim to fleece Johnson when most of Johnson's crew are liquored up in Yellow Fork.'

Webb went to the grulla and levered himself aboard, and when he was clear of the cluster of rocks he waited for Hogan. The foreman pointed questioningly in the direction of home, but Webb hesitated, looking over the now quiet rangeland to where the rustlers had vanished.

'Let's go, Boss,' Hogan urged. 'We can tell the sheriff about the dead man tomorrow.'

'No, Pete. You go back by yourself. I intend riding on to Lazy J.'

'In which case I'm sticking right with you,' Hogan returned blithely.

TEN

A half-mile from the Lazy J headquarters they were challenged by a guard and ordered to throw their hands up.

'And speak your names,' the man behind the rifle said flatly. 'Slick and sharp.'

'Triangle B,' Pete Hogan snorted. 'Your boss must be getting real nervous.'

'Just careful,' was the dry response. 'Ride on ahead to the front of the house. And don't try any tricks.'

Webb curbed his angry impatience. This could well turn out to be a bad move. There was no knowing how Johnson would greet them; no knowing whether they would leave the ranch alive.

'Is your boss at home?' he demanded of the guard.

'You'll see, friend, you'll see. Keep going.'

They walked their horses down an avenue of trees, went under a huge hanging Lazy J sign, and came into the front yard of Johnson's layout. A light gleamed in a window, and the man with the rifle raised his voice.

'Boss, you there?'

It was a minute before the door of the house opened and Will Johnson appeared on the veranda. He stood with his eyes ranging the shadows.

'What's up, Paul? What have we got here?'

'Webb Bannister,' Pete Hogan returned coolly. 'And his foreman.'

'Bannister? By heaven, you've got a nerve all right... Paul, warn the boys. They might have a bunch of cut-throats surrounding the place.'

Pete Hogan emitted a derisive laugh. 'So you know about Skeeter, Will? Is he dead?'

'He's alive, but no thanks to Bannister.'

Johnson had his revolver clutched in his fingers by then, and Webb felt his blood chilling. His own hand was reaching for his gun when Hogan spoke again.

'No need to get het up, Will. No need for insults neither. We're here with some news for you. That is, if you care to listen. It was the boss's idea to see you.'

'Pete I took you for a cowman once,' Johnson said caustically. 'You said you'd quit Triangle B when Bannister sided with the nesters. You could get a job here, or at any ranch in the country. Do you know that he's got a nester girl cached in town – in the hotel?'

'I know. But it doesn't add up the way some folks might think. Webb here aims to marry the girl.'

'The hell you say!'

'Ah, that hit you, Will.'

Webb spoke sharply. 'Johnson, did you sic your men on me tonight? Did you tell Skeeter Flynn to kill me?'

The rancher hesitated for a moment, then, in a low-pitched voice: 'What if I did?'

'Nothing much maybe,' Webb informed him. 'But I'll kill you if you did. Even though you've got the drop on us.'

The rancher drew a rasping breath. He had never witnessed such an exhibition of nerve and temerity. Was this tenderfoot cowman a bluffer, or just plain crazy? He said carefully: 'That was Skeeter's own idea, if you must know. The boys don't take kindly to a renegade of any brand, and a renegade rancher is something few of them can swallow.'

'Where's Skeeter at?' Hogan wanted to know. 'If he's alive I aim to skin him.'

'He's in the doctor's place in town. No call for that kind of talk, Pete. Skeeter's got a chance to pull through.'

Hogan turned to Webb. 'Do you believe him, Boss?'

'Doesn't matter a damn if he does or not,' Johnson snapped. 'And if he's marrying the nester girl I hope she's got better blood than her rustler brother.'

'It's what brought us here, Johnson,' Webb told him. 'When we got back from town we found our stable burning. We were making for here when some bushwhackers began potting at us. One of them went down with a piece of lead in him. But he talked before he cashed. He was riding with Singleton McCall and some other wideloopers. He said they intended raiding your stock tonight.'

For a moment Johnson was too stunned to speak. Then he uttered a curse and thumped down the gallery steps. 'Pete, I hope we're not getting to the point where we can't recognize the truth any more...'

'What the boss says is true. You've tried to walk all over him, Will. But Webb Bannister don't take kindly to being walked on. And he knows a thing or two, in case you never heard. He's a lawyer, and–'

'That'll do, Pete,' Webb interrupted him. 'Johnson can take me or leave me. He can believe me or disbelieve me. But renegade I'm not, mister, and the sooner you understand that the sooner we'll begin to understand each other.'

The Lazy J owner was obviously impressed. He lifted a hand, palm extended. 'Bannister, if I've been wrong about you, I'm sorry.'

'I'm not asking for apologies, Johnson. I just want the right to think for myself. Have you any idea where the rustlers might be tempted to strike?'

'Sure have!' A change came into the cowman's tone and he pushed his Colt away in its sheath. 'We've got a sizable bunch of stock over on the west corner of our graze, all ready for market. The crooks must have been sizing the beeves up. I'll alert the boys. Look ... if you'd care to wait for a while...'

'Mind if Pete and I take a hand in this deal?' Webb queried bluntly.

'Of course I don't. Thanks, Bannister. Pete, I'll–'

'Forget it, Will,' Hogan interrupted him.

When Johnson had disappeared around the corner of the main building Webb turned to his foreman. 'Know where that bunch of cattle is at?'

'Sure I do. But this is none of your mix, Boss. After what he said about you I'd be inclined to let him fry in his own gravy. But here – maybe you're thinking of that Parker *hombre?*'

'I promised his father and sister I'd try to find him, Pete.'

'There you go again – sticking your neck out! That galoot is slated for a bullet or a rope, and nothing anybody does is going to stop him getting what he deserves.'

'Let's go,' Webb suggested quickly. He edged his horse around to leave the yard and Pete Hogan soon shifted after him. Behind them they heard a clamour of voices, then the stamping of horses as the cowhands hurried out to mount up.

'Just hope the Lazy J boys don't take us for rustlers,' Hogan grunted.

They rode out of the avenue and bent into the west. The land ran straight and level for a couple of miles, then took on rugged contours. A dark line of cliffs stretched away on their left; a segment of moon peering curiously over their stark rims.

At the end of half an hour they picked up the hoofbeats of the Lazy J riders in the distance. Hogan pressed another fear on his boss. 'Some of them jaspers would just love the excuse to put a slug in us.'

Webb decided it really was a crazy move. What good could come of butting in on Will Johnson's trouble with cow-thieves? Even if they succeeded in discovering the where-abouts of Jim Parker, what could they do with him – try and talk sense into him? That would be as rewarding as shooting at the moon.

They brought their mounts in at a creek and let them blow and have a short drink. Hogan fished his pipe out and stuck it between his teeth. Both men searched the moon-slivered landscape.

'If my hunch is right we should soon be sighting Johnson's cattle,' the foreman declared musingly. 'Say, I wonder if that Basset gent was just pulling our legs.'

'We'll see,' was all Webb would say. He was thinking feverishly now, wishing there was some way he could extricate Jim Parker. He knew of course that Maureen's brother deserved anything he might get from John-son's men if they caught him. If only the fool could be made to understand the folly of his ways…

They continued presently, hearing the Lazy J crew behind them. The cowhands were breaking up and scattering. Then a new sound could be heard. It drifted out of the west like a low drum-roll of thunder. The significance hit Pete Hogan first and he yelled.

'Cattle on the move right up ahead of us.' His face was pale and taut as he hauled over beside Webb. 'You'd better think of the danger when there's still a chance. We could be cut down with the rustlers, and Johnson need never mention that you warned him and chipped in to help him. Then he'd have you out of his hair for good.'

'I'm seeing it through, Pete,' Webb returned flatly. 'But you're at liberty to head on home if you like.'

'I'm sticking it out then too,' the other flung back at him. 'All right … if you want to get yourself killed, let's go.'

Ten minutes later they were moving in on the flank of the running cattle. Webb fancied he glimpsed a horse and rider out on his left, but he couldn't be sure. He could hear Will Johnson's men closing the gap rapidly. Several short consultations took place between the riders as they tried to determine exactly what was going on.

Then, without warning, pandemonium broke loose.

One instant there was nothing to be seen but dark hides and bobbing rumps, and nothing to be heard but the lowing and blatting of frightened beasts wanting to get away from their tormentors: the next, six-guns were blasting and the night was filled with a muffled drum and roar. Webb probed the shadows for Pete. He spotted him racing madly along the edge of the herd. Then Hogan appeared to rock in his saddle, lose balance altogether, and topple into a well of darkness.

A bunch of cattle whirled towards the foreman. His horse reared and plunged, whistled shrilly and bolted. Webb waited no longer: he spurred the grulla into the mass of dark hides and pounding hooves. The cattle closed around him like the angry waves of an ocean. He palmed his revolver, triggered, then flailed out with his rope. For a heart-stopping moment he lost sight of Pete, but then a cry reached him and he sent the big grulla crashing into a fear-maddened steer. It wheeled and made a furious charge at him, and he shot it in the head and neck, causing it to go into a headlong roll, missing the grulla's legs by inches.

He reached Pete at length, saw him attempting to get to his feet. Another wave of hurtling bodies rushed at them. Webb shouted, leaned out of his saddle. He clawed for Pete's right arm and held on grimly. He spurred his mount and it heaved away with a smooth ripple of powerful muscles, dragging the foreman over the path it was endeavouring to clear.

Free of the heaving sea of bodies, Webb reined down and leaped to the ground. Hogan had fallen back and lay quite still.

'Pete, Pete... Are you all right, old pard?'

'You – damn tenderfoot.' Hogan was trying to sit up, evidently none the worse for his brush with disaster. 'You nearly killed me, dragging me like that.'

Relief flowed over Webb and he emitted a little explosive laugh. But then he saw that Pete had been wounded in the gunfire.

'Where are you hurt?' he demanded hoarsely.

'In the side here. But it's just a scratch.'

'Scratch or not, I'm taking you to Johnson's place.'

'Like blazes you are. Just leave me here. Go and look for Parker. It's what you want, ain't it?'

'The hell with Parker.'

Webb looked away to where the stampeding cattle were pouring across the grassland. Guns still rattled like Chinese crackers. Cattle, rustlers and pursuing cowhands were drifting further westward in a massive tide.

'Can't see your nag, Pete. We'll have to ride double. Think you can make it?'

Hogan begged to be left where he was. He was all right, he declared. Webb paid no heed. He managed to get him to his feet and made him lean against the grulla. He wrapped his fingers around the horn.

'Hold on, old-timer.' He gripped Hogan's legs and heaved him on to the horse's back. Once aboard, Pete was able to settle himself. Webb mounted behind him and squinted at the stars. He glanced towards the west once more. The shooting out there had ceased, but the rumble of running hooves sounded like distant thunder. He sent the grulla into motion, hoping to strike the Lazy J headquarters without too much trouble.

It was almost an hour later when he saw the lights of the buildings. They rode into the front yard at length and the ranch handyman approached them, rifle lifted.

'Who's there?'

'Put that gun away and help me get my

friend into the house. I'm Webb Bannister and this is my foreman.'

'Pete Hogan? Is Pete hurt?'

'Some.'

Between them they carried the wounded rider through to Johnson's parlour and laid him down on a sofa. The handyman took a look at the blood and hurried off for water and bandages. Webb stripped Pete, disregarding his protests. Finally, the lean, muscular torso was bare and he examined the wound.

'Bullet just grazed you,' Webb announced. 'You're lucky.'

Hogan winced when Webb started in to wash the blood away. The handyman looked on approvingly. He had brought bandages and court plaster.

'Pete, old son, you've lost a lot of blood,' he observed.

'Soon make it up, Cal,' Hogan told him. 'Dang it, I'm real glad of the rest.'

An hour later they heard horses galloping in towards the ranch buildings. Will Johnson's voice lifted and his men answered. Horses snorted and blew. Harness jingled noisily. It wasn't long before the Lazy J owner stepped into the room, and Webb's stomach muscles coiled as he speculated on what might have happened to Jim Parker.

'Pete, did you catch a slug?' Johnson bellowed concernedly. 'Is he all right, Bannister?'

Webb explained what had happened. He finished by asking the rancher if he could let him borrow a light wagon to bring Pete home.

'Sure, you can have whatever you want. And thanks for the warning, mister. We made it out there just in time. Scattered the wideloopers to hell and gone.'

'Catch any of them, Will?' Hogan queried as the handyman filled his pipe for him.

'Yeah, we collared one.' Johnson's eyes chilled at the expression on Webb's face. 'Wasn't the Parker hellion,' he said gustily. 'Never saw this joker before in my life.'

'What did you do with him?' This from Pete Hogan again.

'Stretched his blamed neck from a tree, that's what. Left some of the boys with the beeves until daylight.'

Johnson told Webb and Pete they were welcome to spend the night where they were, but both men demurred. 'Like to get home,' Pete said. He looked tired and drawn, but there was no reason to suppose he would not make a complete recovery.

When the buckboard was ready Johnson

helped Webb to bring Hogan out and make him comfortable with a blanket over him. Some of the Lazy J men stood around. They were curious about this promising shift in the relationship between their own outfit and Triangle B.

When Webb tied his horse to the tailgate and mounted the driving seat, Johnson said in a sober manner: 'I'm beholden to you, Bannister.'

'I guess that makes us even,' Webb responded with a thin smile. 'No call to step on each other's toes.'

'Your men don't share that sentiment.'

'I'll talk to them,' Webb promised.

Johnson called so long as Webb put the rig through the gateway and went along the avenue leading to the open range. Pete Hogan didn't talk much on the journey home, just remarked that he never thought a tiger could change its stripes.

'Johnson? He's human under his shirt, just like the rest of us.'

'I wasn't really thinking about Will, Boss. It's kind of funny finding out that you're a gent who can stand on his hind legs and howl.'

'Maybe like the Old Man?' Webb drawled with a touch of sarcasm in his tone.

'The Old Man would be proud of you,' his foreman said simply.

The miles fell away under the wheels of the buckboard, and Webb was glad when at last the Triangle B buildings loomed out of the darkness. No sooner had they halted in the front yard than the cowhands surrounded them to discover what had happened. The reek of whiskey was strong on them from their night out in town.

'A lot of good you drunker jaspers are,' Webb snorted. 'Here, take your foreman and bring him into the house. Handle him like fresh eggs.'

'Hell, Webb, we headed home as soon as we found out you'd bored Skeeter Flynn,' a cowhand told him. 'They set a gun-trap for you and Pete, didn't they?'

'Yes, they did. I'm too tuckered right now for talking, boys. We'll chat later.'

'If only somebody had told us we'd got a gunslinger for a boss,' another man drawled. 'Say, that sure makes a difference.'

Heat lifted through Webb's cheeks and he was grateful for the darkness. Jed wanted to take care of the rig when Pete had been brought into the house, but Webb said he would do the chore himself.

He circled the stable, now a mass of black

ash, and went on to the corral. A night in the open wouldn't hurt the Lazy J horses. He was glad of the breeze that whispered in from the range, glad too of a moment alone to gather his thoughts. It seemed that at last he was beginning to collect some genuine respect from his men. He looked forward to a hot bath and a change of clothing. And maybe a doctor would have to be brought from Yellow Fork for Pete.

He stripped the team horses and turned them loose. And when the corral gate was shut he fished out his tobacco and papers. The papers were damp, but he managed to fashion a cigarette. He was striking a match when something small and hard bored into his spine.

'Move and you're dead, Bannister.'

At first he thought someone was playing a joke, but he soon realized that the man holding the gun was in deadly earnest. He froze, the cigarette falling from his fingers. He turned slowly to confront the ragged figure of Jim Parker. His throat tightened.

'No use in saying you're crazy, Jim. You must know that you are. What are you planning to do now?'

Parker was hatless. His eyes glittered like those of a fox. 'I've brought Single here,

Bannister,' he said in a whisper. 'We got chased over by Lazy J. Single caught a slug.'

Webb stared at him. 'You've brought Mc-Call here? Haven't you done enough damage for one night? You set my stable on fire, didn't you?'

'Just a little fun, Bannister.' Jim glanced quickly around him. 'Start walking for the saddle shed. And no tricks. Single needs water, medicine and stuff. I'm pretty weak myself since stopping that chunk of lead.'

'You're out of your mind.'

'Get going, mister.'

Webb walked slowly towards the shed at the far end of the ranch buildings. Parker's gun kept boring into his back. When they reached the shed Parker kicked the door open. McCall was slumped in a corner; he was breathing heavily.

'Who's that?' the rustler demanded fearfully. 'You should have said who you were, Jim. I damn near drilled you.'

'Take it easy,' Parker told him. 'You see him, Bannister. You'll know what he needs. He's got a bullet somewhere near his stomach. I'm depending on you, Mister. You've got my sister cooped up in Yellow Fork. I don't like that...'

'I'm going to marry her,' Webb said flatly.

'And the sooner you get used to the idea the better.'

'The hell you say! Did I hear you right, Bannister? You – the big rancher – aiming to harness up with a nester's girl?'

'He's only bluffing you, Jim,' McCall snarled. 'Don't swallow that talk. Make him get something to stop this damn bleeding.'

Webb could see the barrel of the gun in the moonlight trickling through the small window. Parker pushed his face closer, a sneer warping his features.

'Know something, big fella – I reckon Single is right. You're just bluffing about Reen.'

'Believe what you like. But you'd better listen to me, Jim. You probably think you're a real curly wolf. But you're not, you know. You're just a little whelp when it comes to the bit. And don't try hitting me, because, so help me, I'll break your back across my knee. Your days are numbered unless you make the only safe move open to you. I promised your father and Maureen that I'd try to find you. I'd like to help you, although, heaven knows, that must make me a prize fool. Anyhow, I'm going to make a suggestion.'

'Now we got a suggestion! You're just hell on fancy words, ain't you, Bannister? Educated, they say. What sort of suggestion?'

'Don't trust him, Jim! Jim, you gonna let me lie here and die while you bargain with a gent that wants to nail your hide to a wall?'

'Shut up, Single,' Parker snapped. 'You're the damndest whiner I ever did listen to. If it was me lying there with a slug in my gut you wouldn't be squealing so loud. Would you now? All right, Bannister, spill the beans. What's on your mind?'

'Come to Yellow Fork with me,' Webb said flatly. 'Give yourself up to the law.'

'Like the old lady out west!'

'And when you've served your time,' Webb went on in the same even monotone, 'look me up here at the ranch. If you want an honest job I'll give you one.'

'He's a liar, Jim. Can't you see that he just wants to get our necks into hemp collars?'

'Sure, he's a liar,' Jim murmured with a thin chuckle. 'Crazy as a coot into the bargain.'

'It's your only chance,' Webb insisted. 'If you don't take it, one of these ranchers is going to get you and do what McCall says. They strung up one of your pards, and Pete and I got another one back in the rocks.'

'Just listen to the big mouth!' McCall whimpered in pain and frustration. 'Why did you bring me here?' he whined at Jim. 'You never told me this gent was a preacher.'

'I'm a lawyer,' Webb informed the wounded man. 'I know what I'm talking about. And I've spent enough time with hard men and gunslingers to pick up a trick or two, even though they call me a tenderfoot.'

'You're no tenderfoot,' Parker cackled. He used his gun barrel to poke his hat off his brow. He appeared amused at something which had just occurred to him. 'Well, what about that now...'

'Jim, you gonna listen to this bird? You're going to play around until somebody comes. Blazes, Jim, do something!'

'Yeah, I reckon I'd better do something, at that, Single. But, you look at it this way, Single: I'm on my own now. I got myself to think about too, don't I? I kinda like this Bannister gent, and I figure he means what he says. You really think you can do something for me, Bannister?'

'I've said I'll do my best for you. But you haven't much time left to make up your mind.'

'But you're doing all this for Reen, mister, and not for me. Ain't that so?'

'If you weren't her brother I'd enjoy

stringing you up myself,' Webb said brutally. 'Who wants the skeleton of a hanged rustler in his cupboard. I'm going to marry your sister, if she'll have me.'

Parker forgot where he was and emitted a loud laugh. 'Single, did you hear that? Ain't he the dangdest galoot you ever did listen to? But, I almost believe you, Bannister, I surely do!'

'Don't listen to him, Jim,' McCall wailed. 'Damn you, I ain't going to let–'

As he spoke, Singleton McCall groped for the gun at his hip. He grabbed it, and was bringing it up when Jim Parker shot him. McCall was lifted off the floor for an instant, then he turned slowly on his side and flopped down, dead before his head came to rest.

Webb had taken the opportunity to claw his own Colt from its holster, and now he and Jim Parker faced each other over gun barrels. The noise had alerted the crew from the bunkhouse, and soon boots were tramping over the yard while voices rose speculatively.

Parker's forehead shone with sweat. His breathing had become hoarse and laboured. The hand clutching his six-shooter wavered slightly, then came up again and steadied.

'Go ahead and shoot,' Webb told him. 'But

remember that I'll shoot you before I cash.'

Some of the cowhands had decided that the saddle-shed was the focal point of the disturbance, and they began closing in. One of them called in a crisp voice.

'Anybody in there? Better come on out if there is...'

A long shudder ran over Jim Parker and he handed his revolver to the tall man in front of him, butt first. 'There you are, Bannister. Do your worst. But I'm not going to crawl.'

'Nobody asked you to crawl.'

Webb opened the door of the saddle-shed and let Parker precede him into the open. 'It's all right, boys. Nothing to worry about. Say, would some of you put the team back in Johnson's buckboard? I've changed my mind about Pete. I'm going to take him to Yellow Fork. Oh, by the way, this is Jim Parker. He has agreed to go to town with me and talk certain matters over with the sheriff. Also, there's a dead man in the shed there. I believe his name is Singleton Mc-Call. I'd better take him along as well. Coming, Jim?'

'Bannister, why don't you come clean and tell your men what they want to know?' Parker growled. 'They can hang me, or shoot me if that's–'

'We'd sure admire to stretch your neck, sonny,' an elderly cowhand butted in. 'But I figure the boss has other plans for you, and I hope you appreciate what he's doing for you. Need somebody to go to town with you, Boss?'

'No, I'll manage fine, Earl. Just help me with Pete and the dead rustler. Parker killed the rustler, and you'd be as well not to condemn him until everything comes out.'

A short time later Webb tooled the wagon down the road to the Yellow Fork trail. Pete Hogan insisted on being propped up beside him. Hogan declared that riding with a dead rustler was no bother to him at all, but bringing a skunk like Jim Parker along was something else again.

Parker was riding close to the wagon, despite the advice Webb had been given to tie him hand and foot and let him travel beside his dead colleague. But Webb had been forced to yield to a demand that two armed cowhands should accompany them as guards.

The cowhands talked a good deal on the journey. They spoke in tones pitched too low for their boss to overhear. They were thoroughly puzzled by the turn of events, but they were pretty confident at this juncture that Webb Bannister knew what he was doing, and that Triangle B was in good hands after all.

Later, when Pete Hogan and Webb began chatting, the cowhands moved in closer, wondering if Pete was set on giving his boss a piece of his mind. However, when boss and foreman shared a hearty laugh, they resumed their positions where they could keep an eye on Jim Parker. They exchanged looks with each other and one of them spat from the side of his mouth.

A little later still, Webb Bannister began whistling a ditty, and the cowhands grinned in the darkness. The Old Man used to whistle like that when he was on his own and believed that no one could hear him.

It might even be that there was an extra rider out there in the shadows somewhere, mounted on a ghostly horse. And if there was, the ghost in the saddle was bound to be grinning to beat all hell.

This Large Print Book, for people
who cannot read normal print,
is published under the auspices of

THE ULVERSCROFT FOUNDATION

... we hope you have enjoyed this book.
Please think for a moment about those
who have worse eyesight than you ...
and are unable to even read or enjoy
Large Print without great difficulty.

You can help them by sending a
donation, large or small, to:

**The Ulverscroft Foundation,
1, The Green, Bradgate Road,
Anstey, Leicestershire, LE7 7FU,
England.**
or request a copy of our brochure for
more details.

The Foundation will use all donations
to assist those people who are visually
impaired and need special attention
with medical research, diagnosis
and treatment.

Thank you very much for your help.